The Fear Bus

Paul Toskiam

This book is a work of fiction. Names, characters, places, and incidents are products of the author's imagination and are used fictitiously. Any resemblance to actual persons, living or dead, events, or locales is entirely coincidental.

This book is not to be used as a source of information or advice. The author and publisher of this novel accept no responsibility for any damage caused by reading this novel.

This novel is intended for adults over the legal age of majority in the country of purchase, and contains scenes that may be shocking to some readers.

Copyright © 2024 by Paul Toskiam.

All rights reserved. No part of this book may be reproduced, distributed, or transmitted in any form or by any means, including photocopying, recording, or other electronic or mechanical methods, actually available or available in the future, without the prior written permission of the author, except in the case of brief quotations embodied in critical reviews and certain other noncommercial uses permitted by copyright law.

Leaving the Office

That evening, it was snowing for Christmas Eve.

For once, the weather matched the clichés of the season in this latitude.

The night had already fallen for several hours. Jane had just finished her workday in a dull office, perched just above a noisy and smelly warehouse, under the meticulous orders of a bullying supervisor. To put it plainly, she did this job to put food on her plate and a roof over her head. Obviously, Jane's boss hadn't authorized her to leave early that evening. He claimed that all the early departure authorizations had already been granted. No luck for Jane. There were clearly favorites in this company.

She was eager to get home. The day had been endless, and her shoulders were heavy with accumulated tension. She could already feel the comforting sensation of her plush couch against her back. She wanted to lose herself in episodes of her favorite series, an old show she was watching for the third consecutive time. The characters, both amusing and twisted, made her laugh every time she watched. She loved the enchanting settings, which made her dream of another world where life's complications seemed distant.

Why did she feel such a pressing need to escape into this fictional universe? Perhaps it allowed her to flee from her almost unbearable questions and anxieties. Her job, her disjointed social life, all of it vanished when she immersed herself in her series.

She already visualized the scene: jumping into her thick wool socks, an anthracite gray – socks for which she hadn't hesitated to spend a tidy sum. They were new, soft, fluffy, and simply perfect for a cozy evening. She imagined the sensation of warm wool enveloping her tired feet. And the crowning touch would be a good, greasy, generous, and comforting hamburger. She smiled at the thought of the first bite, the juicy taste of crispy bacon and melting cheese.

Jane was a brunette in her thirties with an air of mystery. Her long dark hair framed her delicate face, on which her deep green eyes shone. She had that natural charm that captured gazes. She knew she was neither ugly nor pretty. She sometimes dreamt of a version of herself where her beauty would be like a magic wand, opening all the doors of the world, like in her series. But that would be for another life. It wasn't her beauty that set her apart, but her singular style, this way of dressing with nonchalant elegance, often making her a living enigma to her contemporaries.

That day, she was wearing a coat that fell slightly above her knees. It gave her the look of a teenager she loved. Its casual cut and worn fabric gave her a rebellious, almost wild appearance. She hardly cared about fashion conventions, preferring to follow her own path.

Under her coat, she wore an outfit that was both bold and laid-back. A slightly loose top hinted at a bare shoulder, revealing a part of her assumed femininity. Her skinny jeans highlighted her graceful curves, while her big, solid, and sturdy boots seemed to confer an unshakeable confidence.

To perfect her unconventional look, Jane sported an ugly wool Christmas hat. It was trendy among the local bourgeois. So, to give herself a thrill, she wore one too. But the bourgeois sniff each other out. And at work, they interpreted her hat as a misplaced provocation. Yet she had grown attached to that hat. The colorful patterns, depicting reindeers and snowflakes, were in total contradiction with her mysterious personality. This hat added a touch of lightness to her appearance, highlighting her whimsical and unpredictable side.

Like every evening of the workweek, she walked to the bus stop, listening to music on her phone. She arrived at the stop and found no one there. Not surprising given the hour and the date. They must already be home finishing the last preparations for Christmas Eve.

Jane was one of those who, over time and the course of their existence, had learned to hate Christmas.

It happened just like that, one morning, without warning.

One of her friends asked her, "So?"

It seemed like nothing, and Jane didn't pay much attention to it. But that afternoon, her mother, Lisa, asked her, while they were talking about something else on the phone: "So?"

Later that day in the evening, it was her building's caretaker who asked her "So?" as if out of nowhere, during their conversation about the building's renovation. The days and weeks that followed undoubtedly became her "So?" era. Even internet ads and social media were part of the conspiracy. A period that dragged on until, on a whim, Jane decided to raise the drawbridge and barricade herself in her fortress to keep civilization at bay. A decision that left many people stunned in the wake of the tornado, but at least it was her tornado.

"So? When are you going to make up your mind?" meaning "At thirty-five, the time to have your first kid has long since come, my dear Jane!"

Since then, and still not having accepted this mission as perilous as it was full of promises of happiness, she had entered into a, let's say, complicated relationship with Christmas.

Besides, to "make" her first kid, she would first need to find the gentleman who would accept her wool socks and her faux bourgeois hat!

Jane walked a few steps in the silence brought on by the still-falling snow. It was a white Christmas like they hadn't seen in this place for years. It was probably caused by climate change. After so many disruptions, the weather had finally landed on its feet.

She walked to the bus stop and sat on the plastic bench scribbled with dozens of more or less artistic tags. She checked the time. The bus should arrive in five minutes. She sighed and waited, watching the puffs of breath she exhaled. Suddenly, she heard a voice behind her. She jumped. It was a young man, dressed in old clothes, somewhat like a mechanic coming out of the garage. He looked a bit lost. No, she had never seen him here. He must be new in the area because he seemed lost in this industrial zone where all the buildings looked alike.

"Good evening. Are you waiting for the bus?"

"Yes, why?" she asked, removing one of her earbuds.

"Can I keep you company?" he offered.

She scrutinized him from head to toe as if he had just proposed to her. "No, thank you. I prefer to be alone."

"Oh, come on. Don't be so cold. You're very pretty, you know."

"Leave me alone, please."

"Don't be difficult. I'm sure you like compliments."

"You're kind, but I prefer to wait alone," Jane sighed, her tone firm and cutting.

The young man, still smiling, didn't insist. He looked into the distance to see if the bus was coming.

"Don't get on the bus," he advised as he saw Jane putting her earbuds back in.

She thought she had misheard. Yet, she had understood perfectly. Her brain, surprised, just needed a bit of time to process. And also to wonder why this stranger, out of nowhere, was giving her unsolicited advice.

She remained seated there, in this isolated bus stop. Her instinct told her to move from this place. The stranger might have been under the influence of illicit substances and seeking thrills. She stood up to retrace her steps back to her office, to wait until this man, who scared her, left the area. She turned her head all around, but he had disappeared. She couldn't say where he had gone. He was rather cute, in the end. He wasn't really mean. But she really wasn't in the mood for that that evening.

She looked at her watch again and thought the bus should have been there by now. She looked around again but didn't see the stranger and still no bus.

She stood up and walked a few steps with her eyes closed to enjoy the music and the refreshing winter breeze, invigorating for both body and mind.

Jane had been working here for five years and was looking for something else because she was fed up with everything: the place, her mocking colleagues, her boss, the unpredictable transportation, in short, her miserable life. At least, that's how she saw herself. She had studied long and hard, depriving herself, working two food jobs on the side to pay for everything. And for what, ultimately? To find herself in front of a screen all day under the lecherous gaze of a physically repulsive boss. It was a startup that made vibrating orthopedic pillows, to put under the neck to relieve it... or between the thighs, as she had once laughingly said in front of Paul, her nineteen-year-old boss, during a retirement party for a colleague at the end of her career.

She remembered it well. Paul had frozen like a marble statue, with a crooked smile streaking across his face. This image of their pillows used as sex toys seemed to both frustrate and give him ideas, with that smile as frustrated as it was lewd. He never ceased to make more or less explicit advances to her, especially when they found themselves alone in the same place. For once, she was rather pleased with her public outburst.

THE FEAR BUS

The Old Public Bus

The old public bus, of a dark yellow color, moved forward with a disconcerting slowness through the snowy landscape. Its battered appearance bore witness to the years spent enduring the harsh weather, summer and winter alike. The front almost resembled a skull. The peeling paint revealed the beginnings of rust that had taken up residence on its tired body. The windows, once clear, were now opaque in places, and in this season, covered with a fine layer of frost on the edges.

Despite its dismal exterior, the bus continued its progression with a strange grace. As if it was aware of its mission as a faithful transporter, it advanced with determination, almost in silence. The noise of the engine was reduced to a muffled whisper, almost imperceptible, as if it did not want to disturb the tranquility of the surrounding winter.

The bus's wheels sank gently into the fresh snow, leaving deep tracks behind under its weight. It glided over the white blanket that covered the road, as if it had found its natural element in this vast and, that evening, almost pristine activity zone.

The windows, fogged up by the cold, showed no sign of human presence inside. It seemed almost abandoned, a silent ghost moving without a living soul.

The contrast between the slow and fluid movement of the vehicle and the absence of faces behind the windows created a strange and unusual sensation.

The snowflakes swirled around it, giving the impression that it was wrapped in a pristine cocoon. The snow gently accumulated on the roof, forming a white crown that accentuated its solitary and timeless appearance.

The bus, an old metal carcass with faded colors, was indeed empty, like a solitary witness of a forgotten journey on almost deserted pavement. On this Christmas Eve, it seemed to serve no one, perhaps due to the late hour or the isolated location. Only Jane dared to brave the freezing night and board. She spent a few seconds examining the vehicle, a mischievous smile forming on her lips. This run-down bus seemed like the kind of transport that no one would want to take: a wreck on wheels put into service for lack of a better option.

Her gaze then lingered on the driver, a burly man focused on the road ahead with a gloomy expression. His thick white beard, in stark contrast with his stern features, gave him a paradoxical look of a grumpy Santa Claus. The halo of the interior lights accentuated his deep wrinkles and dark complexion, rendering the image almost caricature-like. He, on the other hand, seemed impassive, frozen in a solitude-induced silence. Jane, despite herself, felt a shiver of anticipation run down her spine. This simple bus ride promised perhaps more than she had expected.

The driver paid no attention to Jane's arrival. Neither when she got on, nor when she presented her transport card. He kept his eyes fixed on the road, barely acknowledging her with a nod. His face seemed marked by years and worries, suggesting that, like his bus, he had endured more than one harsh winter. He must have been the only one still willing to drive this old heap of metal.

Jane felt slightly unsettled by this unwelcoming encounter. She timidly approached the driver and attempted to break the ice. "Hello," she said in a hesitant voice, removing her earphones. But the driver remained silent, focusing solely on his task of driving the bus.

Conversation did not seem to be his forte. Jane decided to move on and walked a few steps down the aisle to settle into a seat near the window, hoping that the scenery would offer a pleasant distraction during the ride. She wiped the fog from the window and gazed at the landscape as the bus began to move.

The bus resumed its route, passing through this long parade of empty warehouses and parking lots. Then it entered the city, more lively and illuminated. Jane was lost in her thoughts, letting her mind wander with her daydreams. The gentle sway of the vehicle added a touch of calm to her tumultuous thoughts.

Suddenly, the bus came to an unexpected and abrupt stop.

With a screeching of metal and a pneumatic hiss, the doors opened. The driver, impassive, descended without a word, not even glancing back. Profound perplexity filled Jane as she rose from her seat, trying to make sense of this absurd scene. Why was the bus stopping here where no stop was scheduled?

The driver quickly disappeared from her view, walking briskly as if on a mission. Jane felt a wave of heat in her temples, a sure sign of the rising panic within her. Was this a normal situation? Her eyes scanned the interior of the bus, searching for a reassuring sign.

She resolutely moved toward the front of the bus, hoping to uncover the mystery behind this inexplicable stop. But as she reached the doors, they closed abruptly, halting her momentum.

Her survival instinct immediately kicked in, and she reacted with desperate speed. Without thinking, she rushed to the rear doors of the bus, which remained slightly ajar. However, to her dismay, they too closed brusquely in front of her, as if conspiring against her will to escape. "Dammit!" she exclaimed in a loud cry of intense frustration. She pushed with all her might, her muscles straining to the extreme, hoping against all logic to slip outside. It was in vain.

The metal doors seemed to possess a will of their own, unyielding and impassive to her desperate attempts. Her hands slipped on the cold, unfeeling contour of the doors, each passing second adding weight to the palpable anxiety of powerlessness. She felt a cold shiver run down her spine, the cruel reality of her situation clashing with the surge of her desperation.

For a brief moment, a muted panic swelled within Jane, flooding her mind like an implacable wave. She found herself trapped in this bus, a steel giant now advancing on its own, like a creature that had escaped its master. The few passersby, both privileged and powerless witnesses to this unusual scene, gazed at her without truly seeing, their eyes sliding over her like on an indistinct shadow.

Jane's hands, trembling, clenched around the seat back in front of her, her fingers white from the effort. Her heart pounding wildly, she tried to comprehend the incomprehensible. The streets passed through the fogged windows; an urban labyrinth that seemed to tighten around her frantic heart. Each turn heightened the surreal impression of this situation, both precise and terrifying.

Under the dim light of the streetlights, Jane's face was frozen in an expression of anguish, her features drawn by an invisible force. Her mind, prey to a multitude of conflicting thoughts, oscillated between resignation and the primal instinct to survive. She scrutinized every detail of the bus: the worn seats, the metal bars, the scratched floor, as if each of them held a secret capable of wrenching her from this rolling nightmare.

Every meter traveled amplified her disorientation. The city's contours blurred, becoming indistinct, while her mind desperately sought an escape, a key to tame this monster that was carrying her into the unknown. But the doors remained closed, hermetic, and Jane understood, deep within herself, that her only weapon was her courage and her fierce will to survive.

But what had brought her onto this bus?

The streets rolled by before her, the passersby continuing their lives as if nothing was amiss, oblivious to the strange situation unfolding inside the bus.

Thoughts still clamored in Jane's mind. She felt the pulses of her heart in her temples. What was happening? Why had the bus locked her inside? How was she going to escape this strange trap on wheels?

As the bus continued its route, undeterred, Jane allowed herself to drift into her thoughts. Reminiscences of a past she had long tried to flee suddenly surfaced, emerging from the depths of her memory like fragments of forgotten dreams. The memories, painful and unmerciful, insinuated themselves into her mind, invoking the raw reality of her own vulnerability. Each jolt of the vehicle seemed to revive a facet of her history, plunging her into a whirlwind of emotions she thought she had mastered, but which now surged with unexpected intensity.

She found herself several years back, trapped in a malfunctioning elevator. Claustrophobic panic had enveloped her like an insidious serpent, and the frantic beating of her heart still resonated in her ears like a war drum. Another person, also terrified, had been screaming and frantically pounding the metallic doors, desperately seeking an escape from this nightmarish situation.

The images of this traumatic experience paraded before Jane's eyes, like scenes from an old film in which she was the helpless protagonist. The narrow walls seemed to close in on her, the air growing heavier, almost palpable, compressing her chest. She saw herself again, fighting panic, clinging to a thin thread of reason, trying to focus on her breathing, regulating each inhale and exhale in a desperate effort to calm her frantic mind.

She remembered the striking contrast between the oppressive silence of the elevator and the shrill screams of her companion in misfortune. Each second stretched into eternity, each breath took on the appearance of a last breath. Jane had clung to a mental image of a peaceful place, hoping that this mental escape would grant her the strength needed to overcome the ordeal and await the arrival of rescue.

The memories blended with the present, reinforcing Jane's anxiety in this unfamiliar environment. But she pulled herself together. She had survived that ordeal once, and she could do it again. She recalled the stress management techniques she had learned to cope with her claustrophobia.

She took deep breaths, filling her lungs with fresh air. She closed her eyes for a moment, focusing on the present moment. The sensation of her feet on the bus floor, the slight vibration of the engine beneath her feet. She mentally repeated to herself that she was safe, that she could control her fear.

The flashes of memories slowly faded, and Jane opened her eyes, resolved to face whatever challenges lay ahead. She reminded herself that fear was a powerful adversary, but she also had within her the strength to combat it.

Silence reigned in the cabin, only interrupted by the regular rustle of the engine and the muffled whisper of the tires gliding on the pavement. Jane, immersed in this strange atmosphere, oscillated between a growing fascination and an insidious worry. The landscape rolled by slowly through the windows, enveloped in the soft glow of the city.

She approached the windows, hoping to get a better look at what was happening outside, but the panes, cloaked in thick condensation, only allowed for diffuse glimmers from the decorations to be seen. With a frantic gesture, she started to wipe the mist from one of the windows, her fingers tracing arabesques in the fog. Gradually, the glass cleared, but what she saw beyond the pane seemed both eerily familiar and yet altogether foreign. This street, these houses adorned with light garlands, those blurry figures moving in the winter darkness... none of it reminded her of any place she knew. A dull unease began to creep inside her as she desperately tried to place this unknown location that seemed to evade her memory.

Jane realized at that precise moment that the bus was not following any usual route. It delved into dark, winding alleys where it advanced relentlessly, carving a path and veering away from the bustling city center towards less frequented neighborhoods.

Mystery and apprehension grew in Jane's heart, like dark clouds filling a stormy sky. She yearned fervently for tranquility, not for a terrifying ride on a ghost bus. Who was steering this hijacked vehicle? And most importantly, to what sinister domain was it taking her? She now regretted not having heeded her instinct to rush to the exit earlier when the driver had left the bus. The crucial moment had slipped away, caught off guard. Was the bus remotely controlled by a madman having fun holding her hostage?

Jane tried to call her mother, then her friend Sandra.

Her phone did not pick up a signal, nor a wifi hotspot she could have used during stops at red lights. She restarted her phone several times, but the network remained unreachable. She took photos of the bus cabin and the empty driver's seat, and apprehensively dialed emergency services. She had never called emergency services. But once again, her phone failed to connect her to the outside world.

Jane tried to calm herself and find a way out of the situation. She checked the bus doors again, hoping one of them might open, but they all seemed locked. Panic began to grip her, but she refused to be overtaken by fear.

She carefully scrutinized the interior of the bus, searching for any clue, any sign that might shed light on the mystery or offer a means to communicate with the outside. Her sharp, curious eyes missed no detail. It was then that they landed on an intercom, discreetly fixed near the driver's seat. A glimmer of hope crept into her already troubled mind.

Without wasting a second, she rushed towards the device, her heart pounding in her chest. She reached out a trembling hand towards the button and, after a moment of hesitation, pressed it with determination. Her breath slightly caught by anxiety, she sought to invoke a familiar voice in the oppressive silence of the vehicle.

"Is there anyone there?" she asked, her trembling voice betraying a fragile mixture of hope and uncertainty. "Can you hear me? Please, tell me what is happening!"

The silence that followed her query seemed to stretch indefinitely, each second weighing like an eternity. Her breathing became more labored as she waited anxiously for any response that might illuminate her darkening horizon.

THE FEAR BUS

She had to stay calm and find a way out of this strange journey. The bus continued on its route, carrying her further into the unknown. Around a bend, the intercom crackled.

16

The Voice

Voices rose, almost imperceptible whispers that seemed to come from nowhere. These murmurs, bearing a strange mystery, soon turned into heart-wrenching cries, stifled calls laden with terror and despair. These distant voices echoed in the dark cabin of the bus, filling the air with palpable anxiety. She thought she could discern, amidst this poignant tumult, children calling "Mama" in a haunting, distant echo.

Her heart raced as the ambient cacophony faded, giving way to a deep voice, imbued with undeniable authority, that addressed her. Moments later, this powerful voice resonated through the intercom speakers, chilling her blood with its mere intonation. Jane had always been particularly sensitive to this type of voice, resolutely masculine, which seemed capable of shutting down her thoughts like a kitten scruffed by the neck. She didn't know the underlying reasons for this reaction, but the outcome remained the same.

"Hello Jane..." the voice pronounced through the intercom, in a calm and almost familiar tone, which contrasted strangely with the tension it evoked in her.

This voice scared her, but she was also more than happy to hear it, to finally have contact with someone to try to understand her situation, as painful as it was unexpected.

"I'm alone on the bus. It's moving on its own!" Jane shouted with newfound energy.

The intercom crackled again. The children's voices were present, but more distant. These faint whispers forced her to strain her ears, and she couldn't make out any words from the conversation.

"Stay calm... we are going to give you instructions..." the intercom crackled louder, as if it was suffering from a power surge caused by this powerful voice, almost saturated.

They were going to "give instructions?" Jane felt both reassured to hear a human speaking to her, but these words were far from reassuring.

"Who are you?" she asked, trying to understand whom she was dealing with. She received no response.

The bus continued to move slowly through the afternoon haze. Jane, annoyed, kept wiping the window, which almost immediately clouded over again, forming an impenetrable barrier between her and the outside world. The vehicle seemed strangely hostile, as if it took malicious pleasure in thwarting her already desperate efforts.

She felt the bus brake and come to a halt after a long wait. Wiping the window one more time, she finally saw the reason for the stop: a red light imposing its authority, and a few pedestrians crossing the street, calmly continuing their way on the adjacent sidewalk.

Suddenly, seized by a desperate impulse, Jane began to scream and pound the window with renewed energy. Her cry pierced the cold air, dissipating into impotent and inaudible echoes. Her fists struck the glass relentlessly, to no effect on this cold, inflexible barrier. Refusing to resign herself to such a prison, she instinctively turned her gaze to a small ventilation hatch located above the window. A glimmer of hope was born in her, a possible salvation through this modest passage.

She reached out, desperately trying to open the hatch, but it seemed stuck, frozen by the biting cold. Refusing to give up, Jane began to hit the window with her mobile phone, hoping to attract the attention of the few souls still roaming the deserted sidewalks. After what felt like an eternity, a passerby finally turned his head towards her. Intrigued by the unexpected commotion, he approached to better understand the origin of the tumult.

With a trembling hand, Jane frantically wiped the window, using her fingers to trace the letters "HELP ME" backward on the misty surface. Simultaneously, she tried to mime her distress through urgent and disordered gestures that, though intended to clarify her plight, might just as well make her appear deranged and frantic.

The passerby watched the scene, calmly pulled out his phone, and, smiling, began a conversation as he resumed his walk on the sidewalk, indifferent to the magnitude of Jane's despair. As the bus resumed its movement, the fleeting shadow of this last hope dissolved into the city's cold indifference.

Jane found herself alone again, imprisoned in this glass cage, abandoned by an outside world where everyone seemed to have more important and urgent concerns than hers.

She tried to locate the emergency door release button and rushed towards it. After several vigorous presses, she had to face the fact: the button was probably no longer connected to any circuit.

"Press again, Jane..." the voice taunted with an irritating laugh.

Taken by sudden inspiration, like a flash of hope illuminating her mind, Jane frantically rummaged through her bag. Her fingers wrapped around a set of keys, a symbol of potential freedom. Among the various keys, she grasped the largest one, gripping it firmly between fingers trembling with anxiety. With a determined gesture, she began to trace a line on the window, desperately clinging to the fragile hope of an escape.

The key slipped several times on the damp surface of the window, her hand's movements betraying growing frustration. Concentrated, Jane eventually slowed her movements, pressing all her might on the metal. The screeching sound of the key biting into the glass finally resonated, bringing a glimmer of satisfaction to her weary eyes. This first success infused her with new energy, and she persistently continued, tracing and retracing the same line, seeking to carve as deeply as possible.

The bus continued its unwavering journey, deaf and indifferent to the fierce battle Jane waged against the window.

"Very good idea, Jane..." commented the voice, as if it already knew the outcome of this attempt.

Gently placing the set of keys on the adjacent seat, Jane launched into a series of precise and determined blows, her palms pounding vigorously at the center of the roughly traced circle on the window.

The vibrations echoed through her arms, but she persevered, driven by the hope that each strike brought her closer to the moment when the window would shatter, freeing her from her imaginary chains.

It was then that a surge of daring and ingenuity seized her. She increased the power of her blows by using the heels of her boots, striking with renewed energy. Balancing precariously on one foot, she gripped the seat handles around her to stabilize her movements. Her relentless assault continued for long minutes, which felt like endless hours etched into a distorted sense of time. Each impact resonated throughout her being, infusing her with the fleeting illusion that the window was wavering under the relentless force of her strikes.

"Hit harder, Jane..." encouraged the voice amid a cacophony of static.

Jane persisted with fierce determination, alternating increasingly vigorous blows with her hands and feet, her effort-filled cries resonating like those of a tennis player in the middle of a smash, guided by the indomitable hope of regaining her freedom. Her aching hands pounded the glass, her boots struck with growing intensity. She had become a force of nature, a fiery soul in search of escape, ready to do anything to break the chains that held her captive.

In the throes of this solitary battle, Jane still didn't know if she would succeed, if the window would eventually give in. But it mattered little because she had chosen to fight, to resist the grasp of despair. And in this crucial moment, she discovered within herself an unsuspected strength, a burning flame that ignited her being, giving her the energy needed to defy her fate.

With each blow, each tremor of the window under her assault, Jane forged a new identity within herself, that of an enraged warrior who would not have her freedom taken without warning.

Despite her fierce struggle, she eventually collapsed onto the seat, exhausted, her muscles taut, her reserves of energy depleted. She gazed at her hat, which, by an incredible stroke of fate, had ended up hooked on the handle of the seat in front of her, like a shooting star finding refuge in a branch.

Disheartened and exhausted, Jane delivered one last blow to the circle on the window, and her hand rebounded against her right temple. She'd need more strength than that of an enraged office worker to shatter this window. She was disgusted and filled with anger, but this time, her fury turned inward.

"Here is your first instruction..." the intercom had come back to life.

Jane sprang up hastily and rushed towards the device.

"Stop your nonsense! I'm trapped in this bus, and it's moving on its own. Get me out of here right now, or I'll call the police!" she shouted, each consonant ringing with vigor against her tongue and lips, amplifying the threat in her words.

The intercom replied with a burst of static.

"Do you have reception?" asked the voice, feigning interest in the answer, with a touch of sarcastic laughter.

Jane couldn't believe it. Just hours before Christmas Eve, she found herself taken hostage, trapped in an old, decrepit bus creaking from all sides. She still wondered why, by what inexplicable recklessness, she had decided to board this vehicle without suspicion, and why fate had placed her before an unknown person who cruelly amused himself with her situation from a distance. She thought she had seen it all, experienced it all in life, but this grotesque and exasperating misadventure added, without a doubt, a spectacular chapter to the great book of strangeness and frustrations.

"We will stop in four minutes. A man will board the cabin. He will be injured. You'll have to care for him..." asked the voice calmly, as if reading something, amid a concert of crackling.

Jane looked up at the intercom with disdain. "I didn't understand!" she snapped with a hint of provocation.

The bus took a right-angle turn when, without warning, she was thrown against the entrance door. Her head hit the window with incredible force before she collapsed, dazed and sore. For a moment, she remained there, disoriented, trying to regain her bearings. Her elbows had painfully met the metal walls, while her coccyx had absorbed the full weight of her fall, plunging her even deeper into a grimace of pain.

"Three minutes..." informed the voice.

A wounded man... This situation was becoming increasingly sinister. What could a wounded man possibly be doing in this bus hurtling towards the world's twilight? Jane's only real concern was to position herself as best as she could in front of the door, ready to leap outside, even if it meant knocking over the injured man in the process. When it came to saving her own life, the primal instinct wasn't necessarily to help others. She straightened up by leaning on everything within reach, making her way with determination. Once in place, she intensely focused on the indistinct shapes she could make out on the sidewalk through the foggy door glass. Her piercing gaze scrutinized every shadow, every silhouette, ready to react to the slightest signal.

"Two minutes..." informed the voice mixed with a crackle.

Jane was meticulously crafting her plan, visualizing each evasive movement and their complex sequence, like a seasoned aviator before a flight. Totally absorbed in her concentration, her gaze crossed multiple times with that of her hat hanging from the handle. Nevertheless, she didn't let this distraction divert her from her primary objective. Yet, something insistently captivating made her fixate on it once again. This hat, stoically enduring despite the jolts, seemed like a faithful little animal, abandoned by a neglectful mistress at the roadside.

"One minute..."

In a sudden surge of unexpected tenderness, Jane moved with determination towards the abandoned hat. In just a few steps, she reached it, unhooked it from the handle, and lifted it above her head, as if it were a priceless treasure snatched from the claws of oblivion. Her pride seemed excessive, as if she had just saved a child's life. The hat immediately resumed its rightful place on her head, as if it had always awaited this moment. Her serene face and closed eyes hinted at a deep smile of satisfaction. How could one become attached to a simple piece of wool with such unsightly patterns? Yet, at this precise moment, this hat seemed to embody all the warmth and security in the world.

"Thirty seconds..." indicated the voice.

She returned to the front of the door with a certain ease. She was starting to master the art of moving in this confined and mobile space without the support of the furniture.

The engine changed pitch before the bus came to a complete stop. Jane didn't bother to wipe the door glass to try to see outside. She stood ready, all her muscles tense, ready to channel all her strength to propel herself outside.

The intercom crackled for a long time, as if a voice was about to be heard at any moment, but nothing disturbed Jane's intense concentration.

The hissing of the pneumatic pressure sounded, and the doors opened before her, letting in a cold breeze and a few snowflakes into the bus. This fresh air felt amazing and marked the signal for her frenetic escape.

Jane darted through the gaping door as if catapulted. She rolled on the pavement covered with a thin layer of snow that clung in places to her face. On the ground, she looked at the bus, its door still open, realizing that she had escaped far more easily than she had imagined.

The Christmas night enveloped the small deserted street in a mysterious charm. Shimmering lights sparkled above the empty sidewalks, illuminating the picturesque facades of the houses with lit windows.

Snowflakes danced in the air, gently descending from the sky, creating a fairy-tale landscape. Each unique flake reflected the surrounding colorful lights, adding a soft and ethereal glow to the scene. The silence typical of snow enveloped the street, muffling the usual urban sounds, leaving only a soothing calm.

The street lamps, adorned with festive light garlands, cast delicate shadows on the pristine ground. Their subdued lights created a warm and inviting ambiance, fostering an atmosphere of peace and serenity. The few trees lining the street seemed frozen in time, their branches delicately covered in snow appeared to watch over this Christmas scene with quiet grace.

The silence was interrupted only by the gentle rustling of snowflakes touching the ground, creating a delicate and almost imperceptible symphony. The footsteps of a solitary passerby in the distance, wrapped in a warm coat, echoed in this frozen universe.

Jane slipped slightly where she stood but managed to get back up. She started running with all her might, scanning the surroundings, heading towards the woman.

"Madam! Madam, help me!" she cried out as she approached.

At the moment when the woman turned at the end of the sidewalk, disappearing into the adjacent street, Jane felt a searing pain at the back of her head. Then, it was oblivion.

She had just collapsed to the ground.

THE FEAR BUS

Wounded Man

Jane was in her bed, comfortably settled in the reassuring dimness of her bedroom, a remote control in one hand and a chocolate bar in the other. She was finally enjoying a well-deserved rest, far from the stress and frustrations of everyday life.

Suddenly torn from her comforting reverie, she was thrust into an abrupt reality that defied all logic. The sensations of comfort and tranquility that enveloped her just moments before vanished like a fragile illusion, replaced by unexpected violence and oppressive confusion.

Slaps, dealt by a brutal hand whose strength seemed to come from a parallel world, shook Jane with disconcerting intensity. Her head spun with each impact, awakening a dull pain that persisted at the back of her skull, a cruel reminder of her vulnerability.

In a surge of rebellion, Jane fought back energetically, her arms and legs flailing in a desperate struggle to free herself from her assailant's grip. Words of anger burst from her lips, projecting her frustration and distress into the confined atmosphere of the bus.

"Stop, damn it!" Jane shouted as she struggled.

Gradually, her eyes half-opened, revealing a man. His dominant stature carried a menacing presence. He held her face between his hands, as one would with a disoriented child. His other hand, covered in blood, smeared his wounded abdomen and instinctively clenched to protect himself.

A torrent of emotions overwhelmed Jane, ranging from fear to anger, through compassion. She stood up furiously, violently pushing the stranger who, off balance, ended up on the floor. Reality then struck her with full force: she was still on the bus, inexorably moving toward an unknown destination.

"Hello, Jane... Treat him..." commanded the voice on the intercom.

She jumped as much in surprise as in irritation. She could no longer stand that voice and its arrogant tone.

The wounded man, dressed in an elegant suit and a white shirt now stained by the crimson flow of blood pouring from his abdomen, stood laboriously, his trembling hand pressing the gaping wound. His face, marked by pain and distress, was turned towards Jane with a look of supplication, imploring her mercy.

The man's features, distorted by suffering, betrayed a visibly alarming blood loss. His eyes revealed the desperation to find a glimmer of humanity in Jane, beyond the horror of the situation.

The shreds of fabric of his crumpled suit mingled with the blood, giving his once impeccable silhouette a disconcerting appearance. His weakened body oscillated between a posture of defense and palpable fragility, his life hanging by a thread.

The distress emanating from him was a silent plea, barely audible for some comfort and empathy. Jane could no longer look away from his now glassy eyes that implored her.

The vision of this wounded man, in his elegant and immaculate suit, was a troubling juxtaposition of human fragility and lost dignity. As life slowly ebbed from his veins, he sought a form of miracle in Jane's gaze.

Should she succumb to indifference and do everything to extricate herself from this situation that was beginning to seriously annoy her? Or should she listen to the voice of compassion resonating within her and respond to the intercom's call?

In that fleeting instant, Jane found herself at a crossroads. She knew that offering her help constituted an acceptance of the situation, whereas she didn't accept it at all. Feeling the throbbing pain at the back of her skull, and standing on her two legs before him like a marble tower, she asked:

"Was it you who knocked me out?"

The hand he had on his abdomen loosened, and his eyes closed. That was the only answer Jane would get.

"Treat him... now..." the powerful voice crackled.

"But how am I supposed to treat him? I'm neither a nurse nor a doctor!" she yelled in the direction of the intercom.

"Open the briefcase, and follow the instructions on the screens..." ordered the voice.

Astonished, Jane realized she had completely ignored the briefcase, also stained with blood, placed beside the wounded man's body. This briefcase was a new sight for her. Kneeling, she opened the two zippers and discovered a whole array of surgical tools. Surprised by the very loud sound of the speakers, she looked up at the bus screens and watched a video explaining step-by-step how to treat an abdominal wound. The video was clear and detailed. She only had to use each tool present in the briefcase, carefully numbered to correspond with those in the video. The bus came to a halt as she was putting on gloves, a mask, and a gown after removing her coat and hat.

She had to clean the abdomen, aspirate the blood, inject products in a specific order, disinfect the wound, and proceed to sew it up with a small tool she found incredibly ingenious, almost childlike to use.

While following the instructions diligently, she pondered how she could divert the use of each tool to her advantage in an attempt to escape this improvised operating room on wheels. At times, she chuckled when thinking about the absurdity of the situation. She imagined the look on the police officers' faces or her mother's when she would recount this unbelievable story. It occurred to her that without concrete evidence, no one would believe her. As she performed the procedures, she began to regularly take photos and selfies. Each time, she also cared for the quality of the framing to ensure all useful elements were included in the captured image.

The guy behind the intercom must have really taken her for an idiot. He was probably watching her every move from the start via the multiple cameras embedded in the bus cabin. She also mocked herself. With such quick-wittedness, she would make an excellent private detective.

Yet it was on this terrain that she wanted to progress. A bus, out of service, likely not belonging to the city's public transport, wandering alone, probably remotely controlled by that intercom lunatic, and now this half-dying man she was trying to keep this side of life... No, really, how could she not get into the skin of a cat driven by a suddenly boundless curiosity?

She giggled nervously, catching a small drool string that had escaped to the corner of her mouth. For, weirdly, the fear that knotted her stomach had gradually faded, making way for a surge of vengeance. That wasn't like her at all, vengeance. But her entire body was now demanding it. She wanted an outlet for all her frustrations accumulated silently over the days.

The video stopped, and the bus screens displayed the route directions again, which hadn't been followed for nearly an hour.

"Good job..." congratulated the voice.

Jane smiled, despite herself. Her back was broken, and her shoulders were paralyzed by the effort in this painful position. She would have preferred a more tangible reward. The voice seemed to read her thoughts.

"A reward awaits you in the small pouch of the briefcase..." indicated the voice.

Intrigued, Jane slid a finger into this small pocket she hadn't used until now. She felt something at the bottom but struggled to grab it easily. She took one of the long pairs of scissors and thrust them into the pocket. She pulled out a candy cane, with that typical umbrella handle shape striped with red and white, perfectly wrapped in its shiny, crinkly paper. She stared at this seasonal treat and couldn't hold back an explosive fit of laughter that lasted several tens of seconds, until tears. A candy, that's all she deserved.

"That's enough. Enough playing, Mr. Intercom. You're going to let me off this shitty bus. Otherwise..." she threatened, this time pressing the sharp scissors against the heart of the man she had just operated on.

"Otherwise what, Jane? Are you going to call the police, perhaps?" laughed the voice, adding an echo effect to heighten the mockery.

"If you want him to live, you let me off. Right now!" she ordered with a firmness that surprised even herself.

"There is no way out, Jane..." said the voice in a calm tone.

The bus started up again and resumed its route.

A sense of absurdity gripped Jane as she held the scissors above the wounded man's heart, still unconscious. She felt like an awkward puppet, wielding a sharp tool without knowing what grim design was in store for her. The intercom guy had long understood that Jane would never dare to go through with it. Unlike him, she was chained to social conventions. Her instincts, her mind, everything in her had been shaped to servilely obey the established norms.

Having reached this delicate psychological frontier, Jane felt more than understood the dehumanizing violence that awaited her on the other side. It was a force too great for her. She didn't dare confront it. The mere idea of breaking that barrier defining her and becoming a criminal shook the very foundations of her reason. The consciousness of this taboo gripped her soul, infiltrating every fiber of her being. It was out of reach for her.

She hated dilemmas in general, and this one in particular: trapped between obedience to established rules and the temptation to transgress her limits to act according to her own will and save herself at the disdain of the other, whatever the consequences.

That's where the challenge lied: the fear of consequences.

Fear.

The norms, like invisible chains, once again imprisoned her in a state of oppressive conformity. She put the scissors back and carefully returned them to their place.

Without even needing to say it, the intercom guy was right: she bluffed very poorly.

31

PAUL TOSKIAM

Candy Cane

Defeated, Jane clutched the candy cane's stick between her trembling fingers, twirling its curved, cane-shaped part. Absurdity had crept into her life with unexpected brutality, without any warning.

Lost, drowned in confusion, she felt a desperate need for comfort. At that very moment, while watching the candy cane sway before her, only one face haunted her thoughts: that of Lisa, her mother. She wished her mother's arms could envelop her in reassuring affection, that this embrace would erase her anxieties and transform this chaos into a simple nightmare from which she would soon awaken. But no memory of such an embrace came to her mind. Lisa had never held her for more than two seconds, and this reality hit her hard. Jane became aware of the silent pain she had been carrying within her forever. She wasn't an orphan of her mother, but indeed an orphan of her affection, perhaps even of her love.

Even though she wasn't a mother herself yet, Jane instinctively knew that maternal affection was the only true wealth a child needed. Everything else was just a backdrop in the theater of life. Maternal love was like the heart of a star for a child; it was their source of life.

Bitter tears fell on the candy cane, filled with regret. Perhaps she should have simply said, "Mom, I need your affection." Just that. Perhaps then she could have found peace, and her life would have taken a different turn. Perhaps she would be a mother today, instead of exhausting herself by convincing herself that she didn't need it.

In the absence of tenderness and comfort, the candy cane plunged her into the past, particularly that Christmas Eve which remained ingrained in her memory.

That evening, a silent sadness lingered in the air. The room was bathed in a soft golden glow from the string lights wrapped around a majestic tree standing proudly. The intoxicating scent of resin filled the air, while the glittering balls and suspended stars reflected a magical light. Jane had actively participated in decorating this Christmas tree, and she felt an indescribable pride.

Lisa, dressed in a dark and austere dress, wandered like a shadow in the house. Jane, however, wore a plaid red and white dress, a rustic checkerboard that made her appreciate the magic of Christmas that evening.

Sitting in front of the tree, Jane contemplated her work with serene joy. The presents had not yet arrived; she would discover them in the morning, but her impatience bubbled within her at the thought of the many games she would invent with the much-desired gifts. Suddenly, a feeling of misunderstanding overwhelmed her when she felt the weight of a large bag of colorful candies on her lap. Lisa took the opportunity to whisper, "Santa didn't have time to find your gift, my dear. He said he couldn't come tonight and left this instead," then she walked away in silence.

Jane held this bag like a lifeline in a sea of sweets, but even the sugary sweetness of these candies couldn't erase the bitterness of this moment. The silence ruled the room, only disrupted by her muffled breathing. Her gaze got lost in the flickering lights of the tree, and her tears threatened to flow. The pain of a disappointed wait and the sadness of a Christmas without magic marked this memory like an invisible scar on her heart.

Since that night, Jane carried this open wound within her. Lisa had shattered that magical moment in an instant. And so, the story repeated itself for Jane. The whole universe believed she adored candies, ignoring the more bitter truth hidden beneath this sugary appearance.

THE FEAR BUS

35

Blue Rose

"Hello, Jane... No need to try to record me. I can see you," declared the voice with a hint of mockery.

"I'm not recording you," Jane replied as she quickly put her phone away.

"Even if this bus is outdated, the surveillance system has a zoom feature..."

She glanced up, scrutinizing the small openings concealing the cameras.

"No point in trying to block the cameras, Jane. I will still see you," the voice continued, anticipating Jane's intentions with unsettling precision.

"Who are you?" she asked, without much conviction, more to buy time than with any hope of an answer.

The voice paused, leaving a crackling static in its wake. "That is of no concern to you. If you follow my instructions, you will stay alive."

The final words echoed within Jane as a dark promise. She took the threat very seriously, aware of the danger. However, a strange intuition whispered to her that this individual did not intend to harm her immediately, at least not before accomplishing his dark goal with this bus. For now, he seemed open to conversation. Jane decided to take advantage of this possibility to learn more.

"Do we know each other?" she questioned, hoping to elicit a reaction.

The intercom remained silent.

"I know I'm not here by accident," she attempted, pushing the voice to reveal more.

The silence persisted.

"I know you need me. You knew I would follow your instructions..." she added, trying to provoke her interlocutor.

The voice remained silent for a few moments before resuming in a surprising manner.

"I want to see you naked, Jane..." it murmured, making comprehension difficult due to the sound distortion.

"WHAT?" Jane exclaimed, uncertain if she'd heard correctly.

"I want to see you naked, Jane..." the voice repeated, now unequivocal.

It was the first time she found herself at the mercy of a kidnapper, but she was no stranger to those grim moments where sexual impulses took over reason. Her captor was no exception to this sordid rule.

"You find me attractive then?" she asked, forcing a smile, trying to hide her disgust.

A new wave of static crackled through the intercom, threatening to detach from its housing.

"Very..." the voice responded.

Jane felt flattered, but mostly saddened and tired of only attracting troubled men. There must have been something in her that made them believe they had a chance. Maybe her kindness? Despite a clear misanthropy, she remained that smiling and helpful girl with others. The trouble was that for many unsubtle guys, a smile often meant: "I want to have sex, take me." She decided to play the game, hoping to coax out a clue that would help identify him. Because she knew one thing: when men talk about sex, they often lose their mental faculties. Yet, she was far from imagining the outcome of this conversation.

"Too bad you can only see me through these cameras, isn't it?"

A distorted sigh resonated through the intercom.

"You couldn't even touch the softness of my naked skin..." she continued, mimicking a few sensual gestures with her hand running along the curves of her body.

"...you would be powerless, like a client in front of his camgirl!" she added, increasing the provocation to push her captor to make a mistake. "And I deserve a better reward than this vulgar candy. Don't you think?"

"You are funny, Jane..."

"Pretty and funny... if only all men could see this reality as clearly as you do!" she joked, trying to keep the conversation going.

"We have talked enough, Jane... your next instructions are coming soon," informed the voice, its tone reaching the edge of saturation.

Jane stared at one of the cameras for a few seconds, then began to take off her clothes.

"What are you doing, Jane?" asked the voice, surprised and annoyed.

"You can see it well, can't you? I'm undressing."

"Stop immediately..." ordered the voice, suddenly more authoritative.

"You don't want to see the little tattoo I have at the top of my buttocks?" she teased, feigning playfulness.

"No need, Jane... It's a blue rose..."

Jane stepped back, frightened.

THE FEAR BUS

Two Teenagers

The piercing screams outside the bus abruptly interrupted Jane's thoughts, just as the vehicle had barely come to a stop. With a frantic gesture, she wiped the fogged-up window with the back of her sleeve, desperately trying to discern the source of the cries. However, the windows remained too opaque for her to see anything other than indistinct shapes.

Suddenly, her gaze froze when she saw what seemed to be the silhouettes of two teenagers. They were desperately clinging to the bus doors, one at the front, the other in the middle, their agility evident in a fierce struggle to seek shelter.

Without hesitation, Jane rushed to the nearest door to help them. She gripped the handle firmly and pulled with all her might, fighting against the relentless resistance of the lock. As she pulled inward, the teenagers pushed from the outside, redoubling their efforts with ever-increasing strength.

"Hold on!" she shouted energetically, trying to encourage them.

Her muscles tensed to the extreme as she concentrated all her energy on a desperate attempt to open the stubbornly closed door. Their eyes briefly met through the rubber gap of the double doors, infusing Jane with renewed determination. With one last titanic effort, she managed to open it partially, enough for the two young people to slip inside the bus, one after the other.

"Hurry up, it's going to start again!" she cried, seeing in these unexpected reinforcements a chance to escape her captivity.

An immense relief filled Jane as she welcomed the two teenagers, briefly hugging them in a welcoming embrace that they accepted without hesitation.

"Don't panic, ma'am, we're here to help you," one of the youths explained, his face lit by a satisfied smile.

The bus doors closed loudly, trapping the passengers inside once more.

"Don't play with my nerves, Jane, you might regret it..." a cold voice threatened.

"Who's that?" Lucas asked, straining his ears.

"Don't worry, it's the DJ!" Louis replied with a hint of mischief. "Me, I'm Louis, and he's Lucas," he introduced himself confidently.

Louis and Lucas were two teenagers nearing adulthood, dressed in casual outfits typical of their age. Lucas, with his tousled brown hair, wore a black hoodie and faded jeans, a slight anxiety shining in his eyes. Next to him, Louis, taller, sported a messy blonde mane hidden under a cap he had just taken out of his pocket. He wore a navy blue quilted jacket and canvas trousers, his curious eyes scrutinizing their surroundings vigilantly.

"Nice to meet you, I'm Jane," she introduced herself briefly before hurriedly recounting everything she had just experienced. The two young men exchanged incredulous looks upon discovering the body of an injured man, lying unconscious.

"Who is that?" Louis asked.

"I don't know. Use your phones to call for help!" Jane whispered urgently, watching the bus resume its route.

"We've already called, ma'am. Your bus is trending on social media. Lucas and I wanted to see it in person..." Louis explained, pride sparkling in his eyes for having entered the lair of the villain who seemed to bring unprecedented turmoil to this otherwise monotonous town.

"You want selfies? Is that it?" Jane joked, though the urge to joke was sorely lacking.

"Yes, you don't mind, do you?" Lucas asked with a mischievous smile.

"Later, later. Call again. I need to give all the details to the police!" she urged them, agitated.

Louis hastily pulled out his phone, but disappointment quickly gripped him.

"Ah, no signal, no wifi, damn it!" he exclaimed, dismayed, before asking Lucas to try with his own.

"Nothing either," confirmed Lucas, helpless. The lack of signal began to weigh on him, and he already felt the confinement on the bus eating away at his confidence.

"I can lend you a phone, just to help..." came a mocking voice, accompanied by the usual crackling that Jane no longer paid attention to.

"This noise is unbearable! Is he the madman?" Louis asked.

Jane nodded silently, thereby confirming Louis's suspicions about the tormented nature of their assailant.

"It doesn't matter," he said, frantically searching the floor. "We just need to open the emergency hatch!"

"According to the internet, on this bus model, it's always located at the back. You need to press the button right next to the hatch," Lucas explained.

"WHAT?" Jane screamed. "AN EMERGENCY HATCH?" She gave herself a slap on the forehead, exasperated by her own inattention. "How could I have been so stupid! An emergency hatch, damn it!"

Louis approached to reassure her, placing a calming hand on her shoulder.

"Lucas and I will check it out. Stay here, ma'am. We also need to stop the bus to get out," he added confidently.

Jane remained frozen on the spot, stunned. She could almost imagine the captor delighting in the spectacle of a woman who had ignored such an obvious solution.

"Hatch open!" Louis suddenly shouted from the back of the bus, while Lucas, triumphant, made a victory sign and immortalized the moment with a selfie, the hatch clearly visible in the background.

Louis pulled the hatch cover towards him, but a sudden jolt of the bus violently dislodged him. Thrown together, he and Lucas crashed into the seats before collapsing to the floor. Jane rushed over immediately.

"Damn... What the hell was that?" Louis groaned, spitting blood from his split lip.

"Lucas! Are you okay?" Jane asked, helping the young man to his feet. One of his lower incisors had been severed during the impact, and his mouth was bloody.

"Hold on tight and follow me. I'll take care of it," she offered, heading quickly towards her bag while mentally inventorying its contents.

She treated the two teenagers in turn, meticulously cleaning their wounds and applying appropriate care. As she tended to Louis's split lip, she noticed that the young men seemed to appreciate this improvised nursing session.

"It's better now," murmured Jane, gently spreading a healing ointment on Louis's lip. She then cautiously wrapped a bandage around the wound.

Louis looked at her with gratitude. "It's strange... It's like an ASMR session. Your soft voice, the soothing touch... it's relaxing."

A slight smile appeared on Jane's face, touched by this unexpected compliment. "I'm happy to bring you some comfort. The important thing is that you're getting better."

Lucas, waiting his turn, nodded vigorously. "Yes, it's true! It's like all our worries disappear for a moment while you take care of us. We feel safe with you."

Jane, moved by their sincere words, continued her care with dedication, paying special attention to each of her gestures. The atmosphere became strangely peaceful, lulled by the hum of the engine.

As she finished treating Lucas, she took a moment to observe the two teenagers. Their eyes were filled with gratitude and trust. A unique connection had formed between them in this improvised infirmary.

"I'm glad I can help you," she said softly. "We're going to get out of here together. We're a team now."

Louis and Lucas nodded in approval. Jane even agreed to take the selfies they wanted, regretting only that they couldn't post them immediately.

Suddenly, Louis's phone rang, breaking the tranquility that prevailed. The members of this new team looked at each other, stunned by this unexpected intrusion.

"Pick it up!" Jane asked, filled with hope, while Lucas pulled out his own phone and she frantically searched the floor to retrieve hers stuck between the seats.

"Blocked number...," said Louis, surprised, putting the device to his ear. "Damn! It's the DJ!" he exclaimed after muting the microphone, a hint of perplexity in his voice. "He says if we call anyone, he'll crash the bus..."

"We don't care. He won't do it. His mess has a flaw. He needs me. We must act quickly!" summarized Jane as concisely as possible while dialing the police number on her phone.

The tension rose quickly as Jane waited for the call to go through. "Keep him on the line, talk to him!" she whispered to Louis. She realized in a second that they needed to take advantage of this return of signal to trace the call. The seconds dragged on, the anxiety increasing in the confined air of the bus. Finally, a police voice answered, ready to listen to their story.

Jane quickly described the situation in a low voice. She covered her mouth with one hand, explaining that the kidnapper was on the line on another phone that Louis mimed. She suggested that the jammer used by the assailant was probably malfunctioning. The police officer confirmed that they needed to keep the suspect on the line as long as possible and remain in communication on this second line.

Jane took Louis's phone and handed back his own so he could stay in contact with the police. She then launched into a provocative tirade intended to maintain the hold on the voice.

"So, your toy is broken?" she challenged in an unwavering tone.

Louis, amused, made big gestures for her to mute the microphone.

Jane gave him a regretful grimace which amused Louis even more, strengthening their complicity. "So, your toy is broken?" she repeated.

"What did you do, you little bitch?" insulted the now furious voice.

"Since we're complimenting each other, go fuck yourself, you piece of shit! Hear that? I'll split your tiny asshole till it bursts and bleeds!" Jane shouted with all her might.

Louis and Lucas's eyes widened, shocked as if they had just stumbled upon unsolicited pornographic content. They exchanged bewildered looks, incapable of grasping the reality of the situation.

"The plans have changed, Jane... you're going to die..." the voice sneered before hanging up.

Jane and Louis exchanged their phones again.

"Did you get it?" she asked anxiously.

The officer asked her to wait a few seconds, while Louis and Lucas posted their photos.

"Did you get it?" insisted Jane, her nervousness increasingly palpable.

The officer required yet a few more moments to complete the verifications. Then finally, he spoke again, raising the tension on board the bus like never before.

"Jane, be very careful: the call is coming from the bus..." declared the officer in a voice grave and tinged with palpable concern.

Louis and Lucas watched Jane unravel before them, trembling like a leaf caught in a storm. Fear had gripped her, her movements were jerky, her breathing erratic and rapid. Terror was clearly written on her pale face.

"He's in the bus..." she murmured, her eyes desperately seeking comfort and support from her companions.

Stunned by this revelation, Jane, Louis, and Lucas scanned the interior of the bus, expecting at any moment to see the man with the menacing voice emerge. To add to the anxiety, their eyes fixed on the inert body of an injured man, lying unconscious.

Indecipherable murmurs mingled with strange noises now echoing in the bus cabin. These unsettling sounds grew louder, filling the air with a sinister atmosphere as the bus accelerated. Their glances, alternately panicked and confused, betrayed a complete misunderstanding of the situation.

"What's happening?" inquired the officer, whose voice on the phone now seemed distant.

"We don't know. Help us!" replied Jane, trying to contain her fear but unable to master the tremors that shook her voice.

"It smells like death here..." stammered Louis, his face white with fear.

Sensing an imminent danger, Lucas gripped Jane's arm tightly, his knuckles whitening under the pressure. "We need to get out of here. Something's seriously wrong."

The strange sounds intensified, resonating around them like a discordant symphony of unsettling whispers. Jane felt her heart pounding, while her thoughts mingled in a frightening chaos. Suddenly, a piercing, shrill scream tore through the air, forcing them to cover their ears to dull the searing pain. This scream seemed to emanate from the very interior of the bus, vibrating from within, sending chills of terror through them.

They exchanged terrified looks, feeling the weight of a sinister presence closing in around them.

Driven by a survival impulse and unwilling to face the danger, Louis and Lucas quickly slipped towards the back of the bus, heading for the emergency exit hatch, and disappeared into the night, leaving her to her fate.

"Wait for me!" cried Jane, trying to catch up with them, but she was neither as nimble nor as fast as them. "Don't leave me... you cowards..." she added with a mix of despair and bitterness. The road blurred under her eyes through the open hatch. How had they managed to get out like that without killing themselves, while the bus was still speeding? Glancing at her phone screen, she noticed that the call had dropped and she had no signal.

Where was he hiding?

PAUL TOSKIAM

The Briefing

"I'm not telling you anything you don't already know..." murmured Commander Carl Partol, his deep voice betraying a tension he struggled to hide.

He paced back and forth in front of the entire staff gathered for an impromptu briefing, his face marked by fatigue and worry. His barely audible tone hinted at the gravity of the situation.

"Usually, nothing much happens in our small town, and that's even more true during Christmas Eve. However, this year, we have action..." he continued, intensely staring at the assembly.

"Commander, can you speak up? We can't hear anything in the back," called out one of the officers present in the meeting room, breaking the solemn silence.

Commander Partol, visibly annoyed by the interruption, nonetheless understood that his unease was palpable. A grave expression settled on his face as the evening's events took a more sinister turn in his mind. Igor Kowalski, the town's mayor, had been shot dead while heading home to celebrate Christmas with his family. This tragedy was personal for Carl, as Kowalski and he shared not only a professional relationship but also a long-standing friendship, bonded by a mutual passion for sports cars.

"CAN EVERYONE HEAR ME NOW?" he bellowed, his thunderous voice resonating like a distress bell to assert his authority and discourage any further interruptions.

A heavy silence followed, freezing the audience in collective suspense.

"Good. As you can see from these surveillance videos, we are dealing with a professional. Dressed in black, face covered by a balaclava, offering only his back to the cameras, quick and precise movements, undeniable agility, a startling physical strength, and he chose a quiet moment, with few passersby. The mayor didn't stand a chance. We have some initial reports with bus images on social media; we need to leverage these details fully to retrace the suspect's path. Crucially, a recent contact traced between passengers and the suspect provides us with a lead," Partol explained, using a small laser pointer to highlight certain details in the videos.

He scanned the faces of the audience, desperately searching for a spark of inspiration in his subordinates' eyes.

"Any questions?" he asked, his gaze piercing, with a contained provocation.

"Where is the body, commander?" dared a young policewoman, breaking the tension.

"Ah, someone is paying attention! Excellent question. The body has disappeared! And we have no video of the move. The killer maneuvered in a camera blind spot. We are dealing with a true expert," concluded Partol with a sweeping gesture of his hand, as though he were dispelling the storm clouds in his thoughts.

"Do we have any idea about the motive for the crime?" cautiously inquired another officer.

"It's still too early to tell. We have a specialist in the field. To be honest, I wonder what he's doing here and why he targeted Kowalski..."

"Was there a ransom demand?"

"That's a possibility. Indeed, all clues point to a contract on Kowalski's head. His recent controversial decisions, notably on the closure of the municipal pool, have sparked frustration. But he didn't have known enemies likely to resort to such extremes," analyzed Partol, replaying the surveillance video where the black-clad figure emerged with ruthless efficiency.

"Commander, the killer seems very organized. Could this be a terrorist act?"

"Nothing is ruled out," Commander Partol continued, scratching his chin pensively. "Identifying this individual is our top priority. Establish a perimeter, conduct checks, monitor transportation, catalog phones logged in the area, collect testimonies, even from stray dogs around here. Utilize this crucial hour to profile our attacker. Any questions?"

The assembly remained silent. The briefing was over. Commander Partol wiped sweat droplets from his forehead, heated by urgency and pressure. The evening promised to be calm. He now had to abandon his Christmas Eve plans. The celebration awaiting him was of an entirely different nature.

52

Sabotage

Jane flushed the toilet and exited her bathroom. She took a few steps to return to her bed and resume her series when she found herself facing the injured man.

"My name is Igor," he said in a soft voice.

Igor was a tall, thin man of Slavic origin, with a pointed nose, very white teeth, and large, prominent ears. His hair was a striking, almost golden blond, framing his face like a halo.

His face was marked by distinctive features. His nose had a slightly aquiline tip, giving him a cunning expression. His almond-shaped eyes were highlighted by abundant lashes and eyebrows, giving them an expressive intensity. His gaze captivated attention and could sometimes seem penetrating, revealing a remarkable acuity for observing his surroundings.

He had fine, elegant hands, reminiscent of those of a pianist. His dentition was impeccable, with brilliantly white teeth. His smile was warm, adding to his natural charm. Igor was one of those people you couldn't forget after seeing once.

"I am Jane," she replied, extending her hand to him.

He looked at her hand and managed a smile. He couldn't move as he wished yet. A small spot of blood was seeping through the thick bandage she had placed around his waist.

Jane was burning with the desire to ask him a thousand questions to understand who he was, how he had been so severely injured, and especially why he ended up with her in this bus from another age. However, she had decided to serve only one master in this affair: herself.

"You saved me," Igor thanked with a face full of childlike gratitude.

The bus was slowly climbing the side of a hill, and the engine noise struggled more as the floor inclined slightly.

Since there were still two rolls of bandages and a small bottle of alcohol in the kit, Jane took her time to make a solid, well-soaked compress. Then, rummaging through her own bag, she took out her lighter, a relic from her smoking days. Without a word, she headed towards the driver's cabin, lighting a kind of wick she had prepared on the snow-white compress.

"The intercom freak... Are you there? I have a Christmas present for you. Look... do you like it?" Jane growled in the most provocative tone she could muster.

"Stop!" cried Igor, his head raised as if emerging from the ground.

Jane gave him an amused look. She shrugged and threw the compress over the cabin window.

The compress bounced off the steering wheel, briefly sounding the bus horn, then landed on the driver's seat. Jane watched her work with satisfaction through the cabin window. The flames began to grow faster than she had expected, transforming the seat into a brazier that soon licked the ceiling. She backed up to the middle of the compartment, as the smoke became black and suffocating.

"We're going to die of asphyxiation!" Igor cried again, shaking his head like a puppet.

Jane looked at him, mingling amusement and pity in her expression.

"No, Igor. The doors will open..." she declared in a serene voice, a broad smile on her heavy-lidded face.

As she had imagined, the intercom crackled with all its might, as if it were trying to extinguish the fire from a distance by blowing on it.

"Put that out immediately," demanded the voice, tinged with icy anger.

"Certainly not!" Jane replied, more satisfied than ever with her stratagem. "And if you don't open the doors right away, your friend Igor will end up in flames, and you'll find the engine of this damned bus in orbit!" she continued.

Igor stared at her with an expression of great anger, trying to understand how such an innocuous-looking young woman could be capable of such sabotage.

The fire had ravaged the dashboard, and sparks were flying everywhere in the driver's cabin. Jane knew nothing about mechanics, but given the archaic model of the vehicle, there was no chance it was equipped with an anti-fire shower. Jane began coughing seriously into her sweater, which she had pulled up over her mouth. But she was prouder of herself than ever.

She advanced to the back of the cabin, leaving Igor to his fate, when the bus crashed violently into the rocky side of the road leading up to the hilltop. The crash of metal against rock was deafening. She was thrown forward violently, but managed to grab the handles of the seats with both hands, hanging in the air like a crucified figure, as the bus ended its course against the rock wall. She just had time to see Igor being thrown forward like a missile and bounce off the windshield with a thud.

The bus was on fire at the front, the doors still closed, but most of the windows had shattered during the violent impact. Trying to breathe as little as possible, Jane squeezed herself through one of the windows on the left side and fell onto the road. She immediately got up, her arms, shoulders, and right cheek covered in numerous cuts. She began to run as fast as she could to get away from the bus, which could explode at any moment.

Jane frantically searched for her cellphone in the back pocket of her pants, but it was gone. Looking up, she thought she saw it near the burning bus. Without thinking, she rushed towards the bus, whose front was fiercely ablaze. Anxious from the intense heat and amidst the thick smoke, she found her phone, in poor condition. Luckily, it had exited the bus with her.

She grabbed the phone with trembling hands and checked if it still worked. The screen was cracked, but it seemed on. She was filled with immense relief. This was her only connection to the outside world, her only hope for asking for help.

Jane could still dial numbers. She rapidly dialed the emergency services number and brought the phone to her ear. The reassuring sound of a dial tone echoed, awaiting an answer. She hoped that this time, she could get the help she desperately needed.

Holding her phone tightly, she watched the burning bus and the smoke cloud rising into the night sky on this snowy hill, realizing the gravity of the situation. She couldn't afford to falter now.

As she continued to walk quickly, the emergency services finally answered her call.

"Hello, Jane..." said the voice on the other end of the line.

Without letting the person speak, Jane took a deep breath to calm herself and began to speak in bursts, still walking.

"I'm hurt... a madman kidnapped me... I'm walking on this mountain road... the bus is on fire... there was someone inside... help me please... Can you hear me?" she said in a breathless voice.

There was a brief silence. Jane repeated several times to ensure she was heard.

"I'm not a madman..." replied the voice.

There was no longer any doubt in Jane's mind. She hadn't recognized this voice at first, accustomed to hearing it from an old crackling intercom. Panic gripped her, her heart skipped several beats. Her throat tightened, she began to sweat, seized by a burst of heat. She looked at her phone screen, incredulous and terrified.

"I didn't appreciate your Christmas present either..." continued the voice, echoing with intimidating power.

Jane cut the call and checked if she had dialed the wrong number. But how, even with a misdial, could she end up with this man? How had he hacked into her phone?

She was moving away from the bus, taking care to walk on the roadside, on a downward slope. She redialed the emergency number, her heart pounding wildly. Who would answer this time? Someone picked up.

"Hello, Jane..." echoed the same voice, in a supposedly comforting tone.

She hung up immediately, letting out a scream of terror. Nervously, she looked up her mother's number and made the call with gut-wrenching anxiety. A cold shiver ran down her spine as she cautiously brought the handset to her ear. The dialing tone echoed. Someone picked up.

"Hello, Jane..." the same voice responded.

Her eyes filled with rage, a sinister glint flaming in them, as a panic attack rose within her. With a trembling hand, she grabbed the phone and violently smashed it to the ground, where it shattered with a crash. But that wasn't enough to ease her growing despair.

Taking a ragged breath, she launched into a frantic dance of destruction. Each step was imbued with intense rage as she stomped on the device, as if trying to crush life itself. Each stomp was an outlet for her deep distress.

Yet, her growing frustration couldn't be satisfied with a mere stomping. In an uncontrollable fit of madness, she gathered the mutilated fragments of her precious device and, with a strength she didn't know she possessed, hurled them against the cold and implacable asphalt of the road. The sound of impact echoed, a distorted reflection of her own inner torment.

The phone now lay, scattered in shards of electronic agony. The violence of her actions mirrored her own torment. Her mind sank into a deep darkness. The already heavy atmosphere grew heavier, saturated with the constant fear of the past hours, exhausting, as if the night poured its darkness over her whole tormented being.

She stared at the fragments of the device in front of her. The shards of glass glistened ominously on the asphalt, like the pieces of her own shattered existence. The suffocating anguish overwhelmed her. She was breathing with difficulty.

In that moment of distress, she realized she had never truly had a way to contact the outside world since she had boarded that cursed bus. And her phone was no longer one.

Trying to regain her calm, she continued down the road, leaving the blazing bus behind her. Feeling the urgent need to pee, she crouched quickly on the side of the road, the biting cold of winter making her shiver all over.

Jane walked alone in the darkness of the night, along the edge of that winding road perched on the hillside. The tense atmosphere gave the place a disturbing and mysterious aura. The reduced visibility, limited by the darkness and a slight mist floating in the air, added to the prevailing anxiety. Snow covered the shoulders of the road, making them slippery and dangerously impassable in places.

Silence reigned supreme, only interrupted by the cold wind whistling through the bare trees, adding a lugubrious note to the scene. The city lights twinkled in the distance, like stray stars in the night, capturing Jane's gaze.

Every step she took in this hostile atmosphere seemed heavier, weighing down her heart already filled with anxiety. She felt the cold seizing her, creeping under her clothes and numbing her limbs. Every exhalation formed a cloud of white mist that quickly dissipated in the icy air.

Her gaze sometimes got lost in the surrounding darkness, where she imagined indistinct shapes moving in the blackness. Intermittent creaks could be heard, awakening her senses and arousing in her a constant suspicion.

The cold white lights of the few street lamps contrasted with the warm yellowish glows of the city in the distance. Jane imagined those thousands of people preparing to celebrate a festive evening with family or friends while she struggled, freezing, on this winding road. Those distant lights were both a comforting and terrifying call, seeming so close yet so far away.

Doubling her efforts, Jane quickened her pace, even though she knew she wouldn't get far on foot. Fatigue, and probably exhaustion, would overcome her long before she reached civilization.

Continuing her solitary walk, she fought against her own fears, striving to keep hope in this cold and inhospitable night.

She thought about everything she had just gone through, trying to make sense of what seemed like a waking nightmare. Who was that man on the intercom? How did he know her name? And Igor and his wound? Why her? All these questions collided in her mind, still recovering from the shock of the bus blaze.

Soon, she heard the roar of an engine approaching behind her. Bright headlights pierced through the darkness, illuminating the road ahead of her with a blinding white light. Instinctively, she turned around.

Slowly, a white car emerged from the shadows. Its headlights pierced the darkness like luminous eyes revealing ominous details of the isolated place. The oppressing silence was broken by the dull roar of the engine, like a hungry beast about to pounce on its prey.

Her pulse quickened as she scrutinized the car, desperately searching for clues about its occupants. Each passing second increased her fear and deep sense of vulnerability. The white car descended and approached slowly. The sound of the engine grew louder, drowning out the hurried beating of her heart.

A shiver of apprehension ran through her body as she stood there, frozen in uneasy anticipation. The headlights swept the road, revealing her uncertain fate. In the shadow of the night and the harsh light of those headlights, Jane waved her arms, trying to attract attention.

The white car slowed to a stop on the other side of the road. Jane took a deep breath, hoping to calm her nerves, and crossed the road, her stomach knotted with every step she took towards the vehicle. In front of the car, the driver's window lowered slowly. She struggled to discern the driver in the gloom. In a trembling voice, she asked, "Excuse me, could you drive me to the city? Did you see the burning bus up there?"

A calm voice emanated from the interior: "Yes, I saw the burning bus. I've already alerted the emergency services. Get in the back, I can take you."

The driver opened the rear door, and Jane, reassured by his words, got into the car, closing the door behind her. As she cast a last glance in the rear-view mirror, horror froze her blood. The driver was none other than Igor. Terrified, she tried to hurriedly get out of the car, but realized with dread that the doors were already locked.

"Open the door! Let me out!" she cried, panicked.

An eerie laugh emanated from Igor, who replied in a chilling voice, "Settle down comfortably, Jane. We have a bit of a drive ahead of us."

Her heartbeats accelerated as she realized the magnitude of her nightmare. Her mind and body fought against this logical barrier. What was Igor doing in this car when she had left him almost dying and projected towards the bus's fiery front?

Filled with terror and despair, Jane desperately tried to strangle Igor from the back seat. Her hands clawed the air in a fierce struggle. But suddenly, Igor, reacting with inhuman brutality, bit her thumb violently, causing a searing pain to shoot through her body.

A cry of pain and surprise escaped Jane's lips. She instinctively withdrew her hand, her eyes wide with shock at the violence of the attack. Blood flowed from her gaping wound, adding to the horror of the situation.

Igor, a malevolent smile deforming his face, stared at her with a cruel look. In an explosion of brutality, he punched her violently in the face. The impact resounded in the car's interior, making her consciousness waver and projecting stars in front of her eyes. Jane felt the sharp pain pierce her temples as she buckled, her body folding under the violence of the blow.

As reality distorted around her, Jane fought against the dizziness before slipping into unconsciousness. Her body fell heavily onto the back seat as the white car, after making a U-turn, drove back up the hill, passing the burning bus, carrying Jane towards an unknown fate.

PAUL TOSKIAM

Control Room

The security post bore the scars of time and neglect. The screens, about ten in total, displayed images that were often pixelated and jerky, as if they were gleaming with the agony of technicians long gone. Maps and surveillance videos of Transports Victoria buses played in a loop, their clarity compromised by the passage of years. Keyboards lay idle, covered in a thick layer of dust, dotted with fingerprints. Desks were strewn with abandoned cups and open notebooks, where hastily scribbled notes mingled with food crumbs, completing this tableau of desolation.

The walls, once alive with vitality, were now adorned with faded posters from the tourism office and maps of the bus lines, remnants of a bygone era. A few Christmas garlands hung sadly from the neon lights, adding a touch of festive obsolescence, while a lonely little Christmas tree blinked feebly in one corner, its multicolored LEDs seemingly exhausted.

The room was bathed in semi-darkness, creating an ambiance both mysterious and soporific. Adam, the center chief, a tall, bald, and burly man, periodically blew voluminous clouds of vapor towards the screens in front of him. Beside him, Kevin, his controller of a frailer stature and curly hair, was stubbornly trying to reach level 600 of "Demon Kart" on his handheld gaming console.

Suddenly, Adam noticed something unusual on one of the screens. He began to gesticulate frantically, trying to dispel the cloud of vapor obscuring his view, like a Jedi master using the Force against an invisible threat.

"Come on, clear out!" he shouted, his arms slicing through the air frenetically.

His gesticulations only agitated the atmosphere further, creating a slight breeze without dispersing the mist. Resigned, he leaned toward the screen, scrutinizing the image with intense concentration. After a moment of silence, he leaped from his seat.

"Kevin, damn it, we've lost the 8," exclaimed Adam, still sweeping the air around him.

"Kevin, seriously, put down your console and come here!"

To Kevin, Adam was the very relic of sophistication and elegance from another era. He embodied a universal understanding of fashion subtleties and refinement. His imposing build, like a solid wardrobe, was highlighted by his outfit choices that were as unlikely as an all-you-can-eat buffet at a fast-food joint. His too-small camouflage print t-shirt was the centerpiece of his ensemble, emphasizing each curve, each bump, and each bulge of his body. Who needed to breathe freely when one could look like a sausage ready to burst?

His tight jeans, defying all laws of blood circulation, testified to the heroic struggles he must endure each morning to put them on. Walking with bricks attached to his feet seemed to be no obstacle, as long as it proclaimed how comfortable he was in his own skin. To complete this vision of masculine grace, he couldn't do without his cowboy boots, the ultimate touch of virile masculinity.

His sleek black hair, pulled back into a ponytail, represented a bold choice. One couldn't help but wonder how long it took him each morning to achieve that perfect level of hair tension; he probably used a jack to get that dazzling result.

And that wasn't all. Adam loved to perfect his image with an extra touch of class, through his numerous bracelets on his left wrist. The centerpiece of this collection was a thick black leather cuff, adorned with two straps standing audaciously like shark fins. To top it all off, his thick biker rings, decorated with skulls and dragons, showcased his refined artistic sensitivity. Nothing said "I am a connoisseur of good taste" more than these exuberant accessories that seemed to come from a fairground.

In summary, Kevin saw Adam as the king of modern boors, a shooting star glittering in the firmament of kitsch.

"What? We've lost the 8?" asked Kevin, rolling his chair over to the screens in front of Adam.

"Look at this," said Adam, pointing at the screen impatiently.

"No, I don't see anything," replied Kevin, squinting, his face bathed in the bluish light of the screens in the semi-darkness of the control room.

"Well, you have a damn problem, man. Look carefully there! I have my 7, do you see my damn bus number 7?" said Adam, visibly annoyed.

"Uh, yeah, yeah, I see your 7, it's fine."

"Great, we're making progress. And my 9, do you see my 9?"

"Yeah, yeah, clearly," confirmed Kevin, without really understanding what he was supposed to look for.

"That's great. And do you see my 8?"

"Uh... no... uh..."

"Obviously you don't see my 8, because it's no longer there!" exclaimed Adam, banging his fist on the edge of the desk, making the keyboard bounce.

Kevin stared at him for a moment before risking a remark: "It's like scratch tickets, right?"

Adam stopped short, took a deep breath, then cast a furtive glance at Kevin, a look so dark and menacing it seemed like he was about to hit him.

"And now, what do we do?" asked Kevin, hoping to defuse the tension.

"Well, we're going to look for it, man, we're going to look for it!" replied Adam, taking a long puff from his electronic cigarette.

Kevin stood up and waited for Adam to do the same, but he did not move from his seat.

"I didn't say we were going to look for it NOW. We're going to look for it, cool," clarified Adam, almost completely disappearing behind a thick cloud of white vapor he had just blown out.

Kevin scratched his head, puzzled. "So, what do we do?"

Adam, reappearing once the cloud dissipated, looked at him with a mocking gleam in his eyes. "Don't worry, Miguel is driving. He probably stopped for a pee break. He has a weak bladder. I'll call him to see where he is. By the way, what game are you playing on your console?"

For once, someone was interested in his game, Kevin was about to show the hero he had led to level 599 without spending a penny, just with his fingers, but a call interrupted this moment. Adam's phone rang, and he stared at the screen with the look of someone disturbed in the middle of a crucial mission. It was the police. What did they want at this time?

"Good evening, this is Commander Partol..."

"Ah, good evening Commander. This is Adam Lubert," replied Adam, activating the speakerphone so that Kevin could hear.

"We have a report regarding one of your buses..."

Adam had stood up to respond and was listening with almost religious attention to the authoritative voice of the commander. Kevin, amused, watched his supervisor standing still, rigid as if addressing a deity.

"Ah. Are you sure it's one of ours?" asked Adam, suddenly hesitant.

"Listen, I don't have time for jokes, sir. How many bus companies are there in this damn city?"

"Uh... yes, okay, it's ours."

"That's what I thought. A Transports Victoria, bus number 8, registration unknown..."

"And what happened to it?"

"A neighbor saw it in flames on Grison Hill..."

"Ah... that's why I can't see it on my map. Do you want me to call the fire department?"

"Mr. Lubert, a bit of seriousness! It really looks like you've already started your New Year's Eve celebrations!"

"Uh, no, Commander."

"Christ, what were you doing? Couldn't you have alerted us earlier, as soon as you lost its position? What the hell are you for, damn it?" shouted Commander Partol, an old grouch who didn't appreciate being disturbed to fix others' mistakes.

Adam, suddenly aware of the magnitude of the problem, realized something extraordinary had happened in the city. Totally disoriented, he stiffened, his back arching like a bow ready to shoot an arrow. Kevin watched his transformed boss, knowing the arrow would eventually be aimed at him. Adam wasn't the type to keep his frustration to himself.

After deactivating the speakerphone and listening to Commander Partol's orders, Adam hung up, looking absent. His throat tightened, and he swallowed with difficulty, his gestures becoming mechanical like those of a malfunctioning robot.

"Kevin, we have a problem..." he said in a high-pitched voice, similar to that of a little boy, betraying a palpable fear.

Kevin, dumbfounded, watched his chief transform under the influence of an unknown terror. He almost expected to see him lose control of his bladder.

However, Kevin recalled that mocking someone's distress was neither kind nor respectful. His chief was sensitive and he knew it. He decided to support Adam in this difficult situation, after trying to digest the incredible news.

"Chief, is everything okay?"

"Why didn't you notify me?" asked Adam, baring his teeth and furrowing his brow, his face flushed with rage.

Kevin slowly rolled back on his chair, as Adam advanced, pointing an accusatory finger at him.

"Your mission was simple: watch these screens and alert me at the slightest issue!" shouted Adam, continuing to advance, forcing Kevin to roll back further.

Kevin glanced quickly at his gaming console sitting on the desk.

"Oh, you're slacking off at work, is that it?" yelled Adam, desperately searching for an excuse to shift the blame. "Hand over that thing, damn it!" he continued, pointing at the console.

Kevin, trembling, saw his boss transform into a grotesque, disjointed figure. The features of his face were pulled back by tension, smoothed by a violent wind like a skydiver in free fall.

"The commander wants to be informed of all anomalies in real time!" recited Adam in a theatrical voice, trying to mimic Commander Partol's booming orders.

"That's what we're supposed to do, boss..." Kevin slipped, staring at the floor, unaware of the blunder he had just made.

"Who do you think you are, smartypants?" shouted Adam, pressing his face almost against Kevin's, the air filled with a mango-scented breath.

"My poor boy, I'm afraid my incident report will be severe. You asked for it. Forget any idea of leaving early for the holiday. You're going to spend the night glued to those damn screens. Is that understood?" growled Adam, regaining a more human tone.

Kevin, frozen, gazed at his boss's cowardice and bad faith. Despite his desire to help, he found himself unjustly punished. Thoughtful, he wondered why he had to endure such a boss.

"Okay, kid, in the meantime, go rummage through the fridge and bring the beers. They should be nice and cold by now. We have a plan to prepare. The commander arrives in thirty minutes to inspect our recordings," declared Adam in a surprisingly calm and detached tone.

THE FEAR BUS

Two Children

Jane woke up with a start in front of the screen where her series continued to play. With a swift motion, she pressed the rewind button on the remote and realized she had slept for about twenty minutes. Curiously, she felt as refreshed as if she had had a full night's sleep. Her eyes landed on the chocolate bar next to her on the bed. She had only had time to remove the top of the wrapper without being able to take a single bite. She paused the episode and energetically got up to go freshen up her face. The cool floor under her bare feet surprised her, but she took a few more steps until her feet got used to the temperature. As she was about to open the bathroom door, she tripped over something soft and slightly warmer than the floor. Unbalanced, she tried to catch herself on the armrests of the seats but missed by a hair, ending up sprawled against the seats at the back of the bus.

"Hello Jane..." greeted a kind voice to welcome her along the journey.

The sound was even worse than before. The saturated crackling intermittently disrupted the voice, making it almost painful for the eardrums.

Jane got up, still facing the back of the bus. This time, she held on tightly to avoid falling during the sharp turn. Lowering her eyes, she discovered the lifeless body of a woman on the cold floor.

It was a strikingly beautiful woman lying there, as if asleep. Her refined features added a delicate touch to her appearance. Her serene face with closed eyes gave the impression that she was deeply resting.

She wore an elegant city outfit, highlighting her graceful figure. Her carefully chosen clothes demonstrated an impeccable sense of style. A light pastel green dress hugged her curves, emphasizing her natural femininity. Her crossed legs were clad in heels matching her outfit, adding an aura of elegance to her presence.

Her luminous blonde hair delicately framed her face, accentuating the grace of her neck. Her clear, flawless complexion revealed smooth, well-cared-for skin, further enhancing her radiant beauty.

This vision of grace and charm instilled a sense of calm and serenity in Jane despite the troubling circumstances.

"Who is she?" Jane asked.

"A friend of Igor's. She's resting..." replied the voice in a painfully crackling tone.

Jane found it hard to believe this story. This woman, despite her intact appearance, seemed long dead. She knew nothing about corpses, but something felt off. This suspicion terrified her, and reflexively, she put herself in motion.

She turned towards the front of the bus where Igor was in his place. He waved to her with an inexplicable smile. Without hesitation, Jane ran towards the front of the bus, scrutinizing every corner of the driver's cabin with a piercing gaze.

"We had to fix your mess, Jane..." confirmed the voice, as if addressing a child.

Incredulous, she attempted to force an explanation for a situation that seemed to defy all logic.

"She's injured. She needs help. Where's the medical kit?" she asked, frantically glancing around her.

"It's not important, Jane..." the voice calmly diagnosed. "Here are your instructions..."

"She's bleeding, she needs help! And you, help me instead of standing there like an idiot!" she growled at Igor.

He didn't respond. His smile gradually tensed, betraying growing pain. He held his stomach with one hand, gripping the handle of a seat with the other.

"First, what are you doing here? You knocked me out again, you brute! Are you in cahoots with this madman?" Jane asked, increasingly agitated, glaring at Igor and gesturing towards the front doors of the bus.

"In four minutes, two children will board... they will be hurt... you will have to tend to them, Jane..." announced the voice, in a monotone as if reading from a prompter. The saturated sound buzzed in her ears.

"No... not children..." Jane murmured, unconsciously mimicking the monotone of the interlocutor.

A spate of crackling and metallic noises shook the intercom.

"We don't get to choose, Jane..." justified the voice, fatalistic.

"Who are you? You monster!" Jane screamed, revolted.

Small clicks and a breath resembling a draft emanated from the device.

"You and I are alike, Jane... in three minutes..." murmured the voice, pensively.

"Sadist! Don't drag me into your delusions! You pervert. You're going to suffer in hell!" Jane fumed.

The guy behind the intercom resembled the archetype of a low-grade psychopath from a bad series. He was trying to guilt-trip and cajole her with his pathetic psychological babble. But she wasn't in the mood to be manipulated. He could control his urges if he needed to, but he'd already lost everything else.

"I'm already suffering, Jane... two minutes..." admitted the voice in a stifled laugh.

The bus was slowing down, plunging back into the city's maze. Jane, leaning slightly, glimpsed the multicolored lights dancing on the sidewalks in a hypnotic kaleidoscope. Turning to the side, she caught Igor's disturbing gaze, studying her form intently. A look that unsettled her more than she had imagined.

"Stop ogling and make yourself useful. Go take care of your girlfriend!" she snapped sternly.

"I need to show you something..." mumbled Igor, pointing at his wound, which, despite Jane's attentive care, continued to ooze. He seemed truly pained. She had to manage alone, without flinching. Everyone needed her precious help. She didn't hold it against him. She knew he couldn't do more. Giving him a smile, she indicated that she understood and would assist him as soon as possible.

The bus braked abruptly, traveling several meters before the front doors opened. The idea of taking the opportunity to escape hit hard in her mind, erasing her doubts momentarily. Her mission remained clear: to escape this bus, elude the madman controlling it, and call for help to end this nightmare. She would have to resign herself to abandoning the other passengers, even if everything in her screamed to help them, to better save them later.

The piercing pneumatic sound of the middle doors pulled her out of her thoughts, as a fresh, pure breeze filled the bus.

She rushed towards the doors, ready to escape, but was stopped by an old woman already helping two children climb the bus steps.

"Help me!" pleaded the elderly woman urgently, agitated, trying to place the children inside the vehicle.

"Please take care of them," the woman implored, leaving a case on the bus step as Jane finished helping the two children board, a boy and a girl.

The old woman waved goodbye to Jane before the doors closed and the bus resumed its journey.

"THE CASE! THE CASE!" Jane screamed at the top of her lungs, frantically waving her arms in front of the cameras.

The case was stuck, held vertically in the rubber gap between the closed doors. The bus continued on its way, indifferent to her cries. She grabbed the case with both hands and pulled with all her might. She could feel it slowly slipping towards her. With jerks, she pulled until she finally freed it from the doors. Jane was thrown backward, landing heavily on the floor next to Igor's friend. Her head hit the wall behind her. As she regained her senses, she was struck by a horrific sight. The two children had bloodied necks.

No matter the escape. She would try her chance at the next stop.

The little boy stood there, an air of innocence mingled with curiosity reflected in his big brown eyes. His sweet, baby-faced features, framed by brown locks escaping from his bright red hat, seemed glowing with angelic candor. The hat, snug around his head, let a few bouncy curls escape. Despite the biting cold outside, his skin was rosy, and his small mouth bore a shy smile.

His gray coat, fitted to his small stature, was buttoned up to the collar, giving him a neat appearance that shielded his fragile body from the elements. A fine layer of powdery snow had settled on his shoulders, but he paid it no mind. His hands were encased in white gloves, contrasting with the rest of his winter gear. He looked around, seeming to search for something or someone.

Next to the little boy was the girl, slightly taller than him. Her long, smooth dark brown hair cascaded down to her shoulders. A colorful headband held her locks in place, highlighting her oval face and clear skin. She wore glasses with thin frames, giving her a studious appearance.

Her thick sports tracksuit, a vibrant and dynamic pink, protected her body from the biting cold. It was adorned with colorful patterns and harmonious white lines.

Both of them stood there, eyes wide open, lost in a sea of incomprehension.

"Alice, Gabriel!" Igor exclaimed, his voice choked as he looked up.

The two children, taken aback, turned towards him and observed him for a moment. Noticing Igor's strained smile, their faces darkened with anxiety, and their eyes filled with tears.

"Do you know them?" asked Jane, her curiosity piqued, as she approached.

"Open the case, Jane, these kids need medical attention..." interrupted an authoritative voice, just as Igor was about to speak.

"Murderer! Did you dare do this to these poor children? You are scum!" Jane growled, her words filled with anger aimed at the voice, while she opened the case. She had asked the children to sit near her on a bench, trying to comfort them despite the tense atmosphere.

The explanatory video was already playing on the screens, but Jane knew exactly what she needed to do. The wounds on the children's throats were far more severe than she initially thought. Only a deranged and utterly inhumane being could inflict such suffering on innocent children.

What was he playing at? If she allowed herself to be controlled, the bus could be filled with injured people in just a few hours. What was this macabre journey she was being forced to participate in? Why had this mad criminal chosen her? What was the final destination of this remotely controlled bus? It all seemed to stem from meticulous planning and flawless skill to evade law enforcement. How was it possible to hijack an entire bus and move through the city center without the police intervening within five minutes?

Jane busied herself with cleaning, treating, and bandaging the children's wounds. She had to try to save their lives with her emergency first aid skills. The pressure was immense, but she drew from her inner resources, aware that every second counted for their survival.

"You're doing an excellent job, Jane..." complimented the voice.

"Go to hell!" Jane retorted, not taking her eyes off her hands placed on the children's throats.

"Do you know them?" she asked Igor, who was attentively following each of her precise and delicate gestures, admiringly.

"Yes... Let me introduce you to Alice, my daughter, and Gabriel, my son... I am Igor Kowalski, the mayor," he declared slowly, pointing to each of his children in turn.

"Damn..." Jane whispered, suspending her care movements, her hands trembling.

"Didn't you recognize me?" Igor asked, surprised that his local notoriety hadn't sufficed.

"Do you have a son named Paul?" she asked, dreading the answer.

"Yes, he is my eldest," Igor confirmed.

"He makes cushions?" Jane continued, connecting the dots in her mind.

"Yes, his business is doing quite well," Igor added.

Jane lowered her arms, lost in thought, staring into space.

"Are you alright?" Igor inquired, trying to approach her, supporting himself on the seats despite his injury.

"Paul Kowalski is my boss. We don't get along at all," she admitted, resuming her care.

Igor gave a strained smile, blending the pain of his injury with the complexity of his son's personality.

"He can be difficult... Since his mother's death, our daily life has changed a lot," Igor explained, holding his children's hands to reassure them.

"And her?" Jane asked, pointing to the woman's body.

Igor turned his head and made a grimace to indicate that he didn't know her. Had the madman on the intercom extorted their friendship?

"In the intercom... I heard children's voices calling for their mother..." Jane whispered.

Igor remained pensive.

Jane was not convinced by Igor's explanations. If their family was dysfunctional, it did not excuse Paul's constant assaults. Besides, Igor seemed capable of having a dual personality: violent one minute, appeased the next. Why had he hit her to get her back on this bus? What was the interest if he was himself a victim of this madman?

All these conflicting feelings and unanswered questions jostled in her mind. Now that she had finished bandaging the children and the woman's body remained there, ignored by everyone, her sole objective was to escape. She had given enough for this holiday season. She was ready to do anything to get away.

"Thank you for everything, Jane," Igor whispered in a husky voice, hugging his children.

Alice and Gabriel clung to their father, forming a protective cocoon. Their ragged breaths mingled with their muffled sobs.

"Daddy, we want to see mommy!" Alice and Gabriel pleaded in one voice, haunted by the absence of their mother.

Recoiling in horror, Jane was petrified by these children's voices, the same ones she had heard through the intercom. Igor, kneeling, firmly held his children. Their gaze converged on the woman's body lying against the bus wall.

A visceral terror seized Jane, and her piercing scream made the entire cabin vibrate.

Igor, Alice, and Gabriel turned, their eyes wide with astonishment and incomprehension, frozen by the scream.

The world seemed to collapse under Jane's feet, revealing a macabre deception before her bewildered eyes: the children's voices, Igor's lecherous gaze identical to that of his son Paul, this woman who seemed to be the mother... So many troubling details only accentuated her disorientation.

She turned to the intercom, tears flooding her face, desperately seeking to release the nervous tension that was paralyzing her. The doubts, initially vague and insidious, were morphing into terrifying certainties: Paul Kowalski, that pathetic frustrated boss, had taken control of the bus and was modulating his voice through the device. But how could he know about her blue rose tattoo? It was certainly one of those office friends she thought loyal who had betrayed her confidence, divulging this intimate detail to the pervert.

This monster was decimating his family members one by one, probably in a manic frenzy, turning Jane into a compliant nurse following his morbid orders. Overwhelmed by paralyzing panic, she desperately tried to understand Paul's motives. Why would he want to eliminate his relatives? If he truly wanted them dead, why ask her to treat them? Perhaps he wanted revenge on his father, whom he blamed for his mother's death. She had read that some children, consumed by deep resentments, ended up expressing them violently, too late to contain them. A visceral intuition whispered that a tragic drama had ravaged this family to end up in this situation.

Jane was trapped by an implacable logical wall, as oppressive as the physical bus cabin, and desperately alone. Torn between the madness threatening to engulf her and the terror of her deductions, she sought an exit from this nightmare.

Suddenly, the vehicle turned at a sharp angle, violently throwing all the occupants to the right, adding to the ambient confusion and horror. Jane's hopes shattered against the brutal reality offering no escape.

THE FEAR BUS

True Leaders

Commander Partol had joined, as agreed, Adam and Kevin in the security post of the Transports Victoria bus company.

"Who was driving the 8?" he asked in his deep voice.

Adam looked at Kevin, who stared back at him. This visual ping-pong lasted a good ten seconds, as Adam felt destabilized and guilty from this simple question.

"Have you contacted the driver of bus number 8 recently?" the commander resumed with a hint of relish, twisting the knife in the wound.

Adam threw yet another glance at Kevin, who habitually hunched over himself in such situations.

"Commander... well, actually, the truth is, I was about to call him when I got your call half an hour ago. I..." Adam attempted to justify himself in a small, child-like voice.

"I see. Then stop trying to reach him. We found the body of Miguel Figueira, savagely gutted and throat-slit, in the recyclable waste bins at the end of Rocadour alley."

Recyclable waste... Kevin wondered whether the commander was subtle enough to make such an irreverent joke or if he was simply as dumb as his boots. He couldn't "decide."

"That's not on the route of line 8... What was he doing there?" Kevin asked guilelessly, trying to distract himself.

Commander Partol uncrossed his arms, looked up at the ceiling, and almost slapped his forehead with the palm of his hand.

"Alright. Here's the situation. We have a bus, number 8, which has been hijacked and has been moving around the city since early evening. As I speak, we have multiple consistent reports: it deviated from its route exiting the Moulin industrial zone, made a detour by the mayor's residence, and was found half-burnt midway up Grison hill. We have teams at the mayor's house and his eldest son's place. No one's there. And I doubt they're having a family dinner if you catch my drift…"

"Yes, Commander, we understand very well," Adam confirmed, nudging Kevin.

"Yes, Commander, we absolutely understand what you mean…" Kevin added, keen to please his boss, who returned him a satisfied smile.

"How can we assist you, Commander?" Adam offered.

Commander Partol, a thoroughbred military man, was a spectacle on his own. His short, graying face was framed by a beret tilted askew, adding a touch of controlled whimsy to his imposing presence. His military fatigues, matching Adam's perfectly, created a striking mirror effect. Kevin felt like he was seeing double, as though the two men were from an endangered species.

The commander stood erect like a post, his rigid posture reflecting years of military routines and discipline. Every movement seemed calculated for maximum efficiency, ready to deploy his martial skills by breaking furniture and anything that dared stand in his way. His piercing gaze, combined with his stern and authoritative expression, made him a figure one wouldn't want to interrupt without invitation, let alone contradict.

His spotless and well-fitted fatigues were adorned with various insignia, patches, and medals, affirming his bravery and commitment to the homeland on every square inch of fabric. His shiny black boots, meticulously polished, completed his look, reminding everyone that he was a field man, ready to face the toughest challenges without flinching.

When Commander Partol stood beside Adam, Kevin couldn't help but think that his boss Adam still looked very much like a discount version of Commander Partol.

Unable to contain his hilarity, Kevin began to chuckle, turning in his seat to face his screens. From the corner of his eye, he observed a strange exchange of looks and professional grimaces, a codified language. The commander was asking Adam to explain the laughter. Adam, justifying himself with multiple facial expressions, assured him that he didn't really know, that it was probably nervous, and he begged the commander to excuse his young colleague. But Kevin, his lungs still shaking, couldn't control his hilarity. The burst of laughter, persistent then explosive, erupted, resounding in the room like a detonation, forcing Adam and the commander to step back, surprised by the power of such an outburst from a frail body.

"He has a problem," diagnosed the commander, indicating Kevin with a sharp jaw gesture, before moving closer to Adam.

"Adam, I need your help. The maniac has taken control of a second bus, number 3, another of yours," explained the commander.

Adam looked up energetically, as if he wanted to score a goal.

"The 3?" he asked while checking his screens, though he knew he wouldn't find anything there.

"It's running, normal," Kevin stated, focused on his console.

"That's exactly why we have a big problem, gentlemen. A very big problem. This guy managed to screw up your systems. The 3 is running wild. He's put blinders over your eyes."

"Commander, how do you know it's the 3?" Kevin asked, intrigued.

"We have a bunch of consistent reports. We need to establish a communication via your system and crush it!" declared Commander Partol, slamming his palm on the desk, causing the keyboards to bounce.

"That won't be easy..." added Kevin, pensive, already figuring out how to bypass such a block.

"This guy, unfortunately, is a real computer genius, and we need your skills to break through his security," the commander enunciated with a form of fascination in his voice.

Adam, raising an interested eyebrow, replied, "A computer genius? Well, Commander, you've come to the right place. I'm ready for the challenge. Explain the details."

The commander nodded, his eyes narrowing on Adam. "Perfect. But I warn you: our technical team has already tried to establish a connection with the tools you shared with us. But we failed at every attempt. The system is too locked down. My best guys hit a wall. We need to establish a discreet communication to obtain real-time data. That's where you come in."

Adam, displaying a confident smile, replied, "Very well, Commander. I'll take over and ensure we establish this communication."

"Attention: all this stays between us. Agreed?" imposed the commander, to ensure his team's incompetence wouldn't spread beyond these control room walls.

"Count on me, Commander," reassured Adam, almost giving a proper military salute. "Can you provide me with the technical details of the bus system, as well as your team's previous attempts?" Adam asked, motioning sharply for Kevin to calm down.

Kevin, on the verge of tears again, ran out of the room to try and control his nervous laughter. Adam in a full-blown panic, asking the commander how their own buses worked, was just too much.

Ignoring Kevin, the commander and Adam continued working closely together. They exchanged technical information, discussing strategies and refining their approach. Adam nodded, but his eyebrows furrowed more and more with each nod until they formed a unibrow. When he reached unibrow mode, it was a sign that help was needed. Kevin, who had regained normal breathing, understood they finally needed him.

Kevin weaved between the two men and took charge of the manipulations to try and locate and breach the communication system of the hijacked bus. Adam, sweating, watched him with interest, although in reality, his eyes were simply trying to refocus after all the stress.

Finally, after nearly an hour of intense work, Kevin managed to break through the defenses of the hijacked bus's communication system, establishing a discreet link with it. They now had access to the sound and images inside the vehicle, without the suspect detecting them. The bus was under surveillance.

"We've done it, Commander. I've successfully established a secure communication with the bus. We can now gather the information we need to locate the suspect," Adam declared with a confidence bordering on the ridiculous, motioning again for Kevin to step back.

Commander Partol expressed his gratitude with an almost Shakespearean level of drama: "Thank you, Adam. Your expertise has been invaluable in this operation. Now, we must act quickly to apprehend this public danger threatening the entire city."

Jaded, Kevin returned to his desk, without taking his eyes off the two men; a dark, empty stare. Once he regained some concentration, he couldn't help but remain fascinated by their innate ability to distort reality.

No doubt about it, they were what Kevin would never be: true leaders.

The Mission

Jane's hand froze in front of her slightly open mouth, suspending a popcorn flake in the air between her delicate fingers.

She was captivated by the latest episodes of her series, which plunged her into unbearable suspense. She prayed for a happy ending, where the heroine would finally find the happiness she deserved. Comfortably settled at the back of her bed, surrounded by pillows, she absentmindedly brought the corn petals to her mouth, keeping her eyes glued to the screen. Suddenly, her bed jolted violently, as if it were riding a bull in the middle of a rodeo. The contents of her popcorn bowl flew through the air, spilling like a rain of meteors in front of the television.

Jane got on her knees on the bed, trying to understand what had lifted her so abruptly. But an even more powerful jolt threw her violently against the wall. She sprang out of bed and stumbled to the back of the bus. Without wasting a second, she climbed to the rear window and wiped it quickly with her sleeve. A police truck was pursuing the bus and ramming it, trying to force it off course on this isolated road, outside the city and poorly lit at night.

"This is Commander Partol, stop this bus immediately!" he ordered into the intercom to which Adam and Kevin had just given him access.

Through the opaque windows, Jane looked at the dark mass pushing the bus to the side, on which two men's silhouettes were balancing. She scratched the window with her nails to see better and discovered another police truck ramming the side of the bus forcefully. She was thrown against the middle doors and rebounded off the central bar. She fell to the ground, half unconscious, near the bodies of Igor and the unconscious children.

"I repeat, stop the bus now!" Commander Partol insisted.

Propped up on all fours, Jane found herself face-to-face with Igor. Her heart skipped a beat seeing him in this state. Igor's eyes were closed, his skin a worrying pale shade that was turning almost purple. Jane heard footsteps on the roof of the bus. They were moving towards the front.

She got up and advanced, gripping firmly with each step to reach the intercom without falling. "Help me! Please! Help me!" she implored almost in front of the intercom.

"Who are you?" the commander asked, his voice resonating clearly without crackling or saturation, which gave Jane a bit of hope.

"It's Jane! I'm trapped in this bus!" she shouted even louder, hoping to be heard despite the roar of the full-throttle engine.

"Stop the bus immediately!" ordered the commander, visibly annoyed.

"I can't! I'm not driving the bus!" she screamed, doing her best to be heard over the deafening noise.

The commander uttered a few more words, but Jane didn't have time to understand them. The bus braked sharply, sliding forward. Taken by surprise, Jane was thrown against the windshield, desperately trying to catch herself with her arms in the air. That's when she saw two silhouettes falling in front of the vehicle. Before she could realize what was happening, the police truck violently hit the rear of the bus, sending it into a rapid slide. The bus rolled over the two silhouettes that had just fallen from the roof.

Amid the chaos, the bus veered diagonally on the road, pushing the following truck onto the roadside. The slide continued for a few terrifying seconds until the bus regained a position aligned with the road and the engine roared again.

Jane was shocked by this series of tragic events that had unfolded in an instant. She looked, horrified, at the scene before her. Two large blood stains slid on the windshield, leaving the outlines of the silhouettes' heads.

Heart pounding, she wondered what was really happening.

"Hello, Jane..." said the voice in a barrage of crackles and sharp noises.

She stared at the intercom with a feeling of disgust mingled with scorn.

"Why are you doing all this, Paul?" she asked, breathless. "And where are you hiding? You're in this bus with me, I know it!"

A burst of static came from the intercom, followed by the voice declaring slowly, enunciating each word: "I am not Paul..."

"Stop lying, Paul, it's useless now," she said, catching her breath.

The intercom crackled and she heard slow breathing.

"You wanted to punish your family for not loving you. And you wanted to screw me, Paul. You wanted to screw me? You should have just asked," she continued, trying to summarize what she had understood.

"I AM THE ONE WHO'S GOING TO SCREW YOU! Stop this bus immediately! My men will shoot!" shouted Commander Partol into the intercom.

Commander Partol was clinging to the front passenger seat of the truck, following the bus closely. Despite his seatbelt, he held on to the handle above the window to avoid being jostled on his seat. His eyes fell on Adam and Kevin at the back, dressed in assault gear.

"Your crap isn't working!" he grumbled, emphasizing his point with a death gesture.

Adam looked at Kevin, who looked at Partol. "You just spoke to her..." he tried to justify.

"Don't play with me, kid. Your crap works one time out of four. I've got no video. I've got two men in mush. Find something, quick!" ordered Partol, his eyes filled with fury, before turning back to the road.

"What if we shoot the bus tires?" suggested Adam, eager to help.

"Adam, don't try to tell me how to do my job!" growled the commander, not taking his eyes off the road.

He grabbed the radio handset and communicated with the second truck, which seemed to have managed to get back on the road after skidding onto the roadside.

With their helmets and too-small bulletproof vests, Adam and Kevin looked like guests at a costume party. The kind of guests who had taken the theme very seriously and wanted to push realism to the extreme to impress everyone, but who were actually the nerdiest at the party. Kevin was frantically typing on his laptop while Adam, staring at the screen with furrowed brows, scratched his helmet.

Their truck struck the bus's rear again. Adam and Kevin were thrown toward the grille separating them from the driver's seat. They bounced back and fell to the floor of the rear compartment, like potatoes falling out of their sack at the market stall. After the previous jolts, Kevin had now gotten used to these amusement ride-like shocks and kept his laptop firmly pressed against him.

"The old man is out of ideas..." he commented, meeting the tired gaze of his boss Adam, seeking a semblance of camaraderie.

"He knows what he's doing. We have to trust him," Adam tried to reassure, cutting short any brotherhood, as Kevin rolled his eyes to the ceiling.

"So, what've we got behind us?" asked the commander, putting the radio handset down.

"Commander, Kevin is working at high speed to find a solution, I..."

"Adam, in ten minutes we'll be entering Bellevue village. It so happens that my old mother lives in Bellevue. You got the picture, Adam?" interrupted the commander provocatively.

"Yes, I see the picture very clearly, commander... Kevin, did you hear what the commander said? We need to find a solution quickly.

How's your work going on your laptop?" he said, turning to Kevin with an unconscious posture of supplication.

"No. I've got nothing, boss," stated Kevin, almost with satisfaction.

The three men exchanged puzzled looks for long seconds as the truck was shaken by the roughness of the small country road. It was a sort of staring contest to determine which of them would be the most incapable of finding a way to stop this speeding bus without risking causing damage throughout the region. Amused but still impressed by the commander's blank expression and glassy eye, Kevin proposed a solution that had been in front of them since the beginning of the mission.

"We could use this drone, right?" he suggested, pointing to a piece of equipment that looked brand new and barely used.

The anxiety gradually spread across the commander's face like a dark shadow.

He shook his head, explaining why they couldn't opt for that solution.

"Unfortunately, Kevin, we're short-staffed tonight. We don't have a drone pilot available for another good hour. I can't take additional risks using this device without a qualified professional."

Kevin, determined, mainly thought it would be fun to pilot a military drone at least once in his life. This excitement was easily visible in his wide eyes and ear-to-ear grin.

"I can try," said Kevin, as if he had done it all his life.

The commander frowned, a look of terror crossing his face.

"I've always been good with new technologies. This seems like our only chance to end this chase," added Kevin, a skilled negotiator.

The commander thought long and hard, frowning even harder, almost reaching a unibrow, much like Adam. With his last words, Kevin had scored decisive points. However, as an experienced strategist, Commander Partol meticulously evaluated the risks and potential benefits of this idea. Besides, his experience allowed him to immediately sense a man's determination to accomplish a task. He was rarely wrong about a man of action's resolve. But more than anything, he didn't want to end up crashing the mission right in the center of Bellevue. Time was running out, and he knew he had few options left.

"Alright, but be careful. You must be extremely cautious and stay focused. We only have one chance," murmured the commander, as if speaking to himself.

Adam's face remained frozen like a photograph. The level of pressure in this situation was entirely unfamiliar to him. "One chance...", these words echoed repeatedly in his mind. Obviously, he wasn't a soldier trained to withstand this type of tension. But the way he had immobilized himself, not even breathing, made one fear for his health.

"Boss, are you okay?" Kevin asked out of human compassion.

"Adam, is everything alright?" the commander reiterated, tapping on the fence to draw the stone man's attention.

Adam eventually turned his head and resumed more natural movements, seeking his breath as if emerging from a deep dive.

Commander Partol gave Kevin the go-ahead with a firm nod of his jaw. Kevin nodded back with a confident smile. He knew he was venturing into the unknown, but it was their only glimmer of hope. They quickly put their plan into action. Kevin unpacked the device while entering the unlock code provided by the commander. He checked the battery levels and handed one control screen to the commander through the small sliding hatch in the fence and another to his boss, Adam. But Adam lay unconscious on the bench.

The commander and Kevin exchanged a complicit smile, ensuring Adam remained securely strapped to the bench until his "return."

Kevin quickly took control of the drone with a skill that surprised even himself, then flew it discreetly in front of the truck and then to the bus.

"Try the emergency hatch at the back, kid. The children might have left it open," suggested the commander, gesticulating like a ground crewman guiding an airplane, already contemplating what excuse he might give his superiors if the mission failed.

Jane moved from window to window, trying to understand where the shrill noise outside was coming from. She kept wiping one window after another but saw nothing conclusive.

"A drone is approaching..." informed a voice.

"Where?" asked Jane, surprised at her own reaction, as if she were teaming up with her captor.

The commander and Kevin remained intensely focused on the images the drone was sending back. The device moved slowly under the bus until it located an opening into the cabin.

"I FOUND IT!" Kevin exclaimed upon discovering that the emergency hatch at the back of the bus was indeed left open.

His shout brought Adam back to consciousness. He straightened up on the bench and stretched as if he had just had a very good night's sleep.

Eyes fixed on his screen, the commander murmured his instructions: "Climb... climb... now move forward... forward... a little more..."

A silence settled between the two men when the interior of the bus littered with corpses was revealed to them on the control screens.

"This is... it's horrific," stammered Kevin, sweating.

"Don't look at the floor, kid. Focus on her!" ordered the commander, grimacing himself.

"We need to call for help from another team," tried Kevin, struggling to hold back a deep revulsion and a sudden urge to vomit.

"The other team is us! This is no time to falter. Stay focused!" insisted the commander, wiping the sweat-soaked forehead.

Jane suddenly appeared on the control screens. She had just turned around and was facing the drone.

Adam, close to Kevin's screen, adjusted his headset to better follow the scene.

"FIRE! FIRE NOW!" ordered the commander, performing his infamous execution gesture.

Surprised by this unexpected command, Kevin momentarily lost control of the drone, which started to zigzag inside the bus cabin.

Adam, overcome by another panic attack upon hearing this martial order, collapsed heavily to the ground. Kevin observed his boss's noisy fall out of the corner of his eye.

"PAY ATTENTION!" shouted the commander as he saw the drone lurch. "Don't worry about him. Aim and shoot. Now!" he repeated vehemently.

Kevin began to sweat profusely. He had not planned to use the drone in this manner at all. What he had imagined to be a life-sized video game was turning into a real military operation.

"Commander, I'm not sure I can do this," admitted Kevin. His forehead was drenched with sweat. His trembling voice nearly choked. "I want to help, but I can't hurt someone," he added, feeling dazed.

The commander understood Kevin's feelings and knew this situation was difficult for a young man accustomed to monitoring bus routes. He took a deep breath and said in a calm voice: "This is our only option. Don't waste it."

The pressure was immense in Kevin's mind. This situation was a first for him, who usually purred with boredom in front of his screens, waiting for his shift to end. He knew this tipping point could change many things, including his own life. He looked at Jane again through the drone's camera. She was still unaware of the danger looming over her. He knew that time was scarce and every second counted.

"Kevin," continued the commander in his most gentle and reassuring voice, starkly contrasting with his usual authoritative barks, "we need to act now. If we wait any longer, the situation could become even more dangerous."

Kevin hesitated for a moment longer, thoughts swirling in his mind, then made a difficult decision. He knew he had to trust the commander. "I'll try to neutralize her without harming her," he replied, gradually regaining his courage and a calmer breath.

Commander Partol realized at that precise moment that the situation had slipped out of his control. Out of options, he had entrusted the most critical part of the assault to this young man, fully aware that the latter would hesitate to use the drone's weapon. Deep down, he knew this was a risk.

Heart pounding, Kevin adjusted the drone's controls to stabilize it and approach Jane slowly. He desperately searched for a way to disarm her without using excessive force.

As the drone silently approached, an idea sparked in Kevin's mind. He could use the compressed air shot loaded with paralytic. This would allow him to create a gust around Jane, powerful enough to disorient her without causing harm.

"I'll use the paralytic spray," informed Kevin, very focused, while the commander nodded in agreement.

With incredible precision, Kevin activated the drone's mechanism, releasing a jet of compressed air towards Jane. The gust blew around her, causing her to step back a few steps. She fixed her gaze on the flying machine, trying to comprehend what had just happened.

"DESTROY THAT DRONE..." ordered the voice, more garbled with static than ever, making the words barely discernible.

Jane was terrified, at her wit's end, struggling to hold back desperate sobs. She turned towards the drone, ignoring the malicious voice's commands.

"Help me, I beg you, help me!" she implored in a trembling voice, full of despair.

94

Christmas Meal

Jade hadn't even realized she had just finished an entire bar of chocolate. After the immediate pleasure, her gluttony gave way to that cold guilt of having invited three extra pounds into her life. She wasn't exactly sure how much, but that's what she imagined. However, she knew there would be consequences. And those consequences, like all the great irrational chocolate lovers, she hated. Very aware of the suffering in this world, particularly hunger, she also felt guilty for having the luxury to devour a bar in one go and do it again the next day if she felt like it. In short, her relationship with chocolate was quite complicated.

Jane hadn't even realized she had just finished an entire chocolate bar. After the immediate pleasure, she was left with the cold guilt of having invited three more kilos into her life. She didn't know exactly how much weight she'd gained, but that's what she imagined. She knew, however, that there would be consequences. And those consequences, like all great irrational chocolate lovers, she hated them. Very conscious of the suffering in this world, especially famine, she also felt guilty for having the luxury of devouring a whole bar in one go and repeating the experience the next day if she felt like it. In short, her relationship with chocolate was the most complicated.

Jane got up from her bed, where she had been comfortably installed, in search of a bottle of water to rinse her mouth. But as soon as she set foot on the ground, she was struck by violent dizziness that made her stagger all along the dark corridor of the bus, before ending her course, half sprawling, between the back bench and the floor.

The pains at the back of her head and all over her face around her mouth brought her back brutally to this reality, without any chocolate bar.

She got up with difficulty and long contemplated this new vehicle, waiting for the dizziness to dissipate. Clumsily, she observed her own body, her arms, and hands. She now wore a long black dress, a bit slit on the side, and stilettos that pinched her toes. Her hair was styled in a bun, and her nails were manicured with undeniable skill. As she lifted her head with the help of an arm, she jolted backward, falling back onto the floor. The inside of the bus had just lit up with a thousand lights, and an introductory video began on all the screens, the sound at full volume.

"Welcome to this modern and luxurious bus, transformed into a true winter paradise for the Christmas holidays! Upon entering, you will be immediately struck by the magical atmosphere that reigns here.

The seats, of exceptional comfort, are dressed in a soft and plush fabric, harmoniously matched with touches of red and green, thus evoking the traditional colors of Christmas. Each seat is adorned with finely crafted wooden armrests, adding a touch of elegance and sophistication.

The floor is covered with real parquet, as soft as a cloud, which will provide you with absolute comfort with each of your steps. This parquet is engraved with an enchanting winter pattern, with snowflakes and stars, transporting your imagination to snowy landscapes.

The windows, real Christmas tableaux, are adorned with enchanted decorations. Delicate stickers, representing snowflakes and snowmen, adorn the panes, while small string lights, skillfully arranged around the frames, emit a festive glow outside.

The ceiling is decorated with dazzling luminous suspensions, creating a celestial and majestic effect. These sparkling lights emit a soft aura, giving the bus interior one of the most fairy-tale-like atmospheres.

Huge, beautifully framed Christmas posters embellish the bus walls. They transport you to picturesque winter scenes, where love, joy, and the conviviality typical of this enchanting time of the year reign.

To complete this sensory experience, a sweet and captivating melody, typical of the Christmas holidays, discreetly escapes from the speakers, creating a harmonious and comforting ambiance.

This modern, luxurious public bus, carefully decorated for the Christmas holidays, offers you a unique opportunity to enjoy a peaceful and comfortable journey while enveloping you in the magical and warm spirit of this wonderful season."

Jane was stunned, both literally and figuratively. It was no longer a bus offered to her, still sitting on the floor, but a rolling amusement park in glory of Christmas. Those red and green colors, those flashing lights, those gift boxes placed here and there, those quaint music accompanied by bells and sleigh sounds... Only Santa Claus himself was missing to perfect this atmosphere.

With an energetic gesture, she removed the bandage that had been stuck on her nose and tried to see outside this new universe. She was quickly interrupted.

"Hello Jane..." said the voice, this time without any crackle and with crystal clarity. This new voice filled every cubic centimeter of the cabin, in a deep, powerful, and warm manner, as if it sought to soothe Jane's soul with each word spoken.

For a moment, Jane thought she was dealing with a bus enthusiast. Then she realized that the vehicle was no longer moving. It was stationary, somewhere she couldn't identify. All windows were covered with decorations, and all she could perceive outside was a thick, inscrutable darkness. She thought her captor had likely made all these decoration efforts to seek forgiveness. Vain efforts in her eyes, as she hated this celebration which she also considered vulgar and commercially obscene.

She approached the small table, leaned against the bus wall and magnificently decorated. Despite herself, she was amazed by the sight of the sumptuous cutlery shining in the flickering candle light. She settled gracefully into the comfortable chair reserved for her.

The voice, tinged with excitement, invited her: "Welcome, Jane, to this Christmas meal. We've prepared a feast worthy of the most special occasions. Let yourself be pampered and enjoy every moment of this magical time."

Stunned, she stared at the screens showing the details of a Christmas feast. She had trouble understanding this staging and felt awkward and disconcerted.

"You look splendid tonight, Jane..." complimented the voice, showing images of her. She then realized she was dressed and groomed like a princess, which made her even more uncomfortable, not knowing what to do with her hands or her body.

A hatch opened on the side, and a tray loaded with delicious appetizers slid to the center of the table. Jane observed them, sniffed them from a distance, then, tempted by their appetizing appearance, savored them with delight. The exquisite flavors exploded in her mouth, offering her a foretaste of the delicacies to come.

The voice, now musical and enchanting, resumed: "Our talented chefs have crafted a spectacular menu for you tonight, Jane. Prepare to be transported by refined dishes and harmonious flavors that will awaken all your senses."

The first dish was removed, and a second slid to the center of the table. A mixture of aromas and colors dazzled Jane. She discovered with wonder an assortment of delicate dishes: fresh and fragrant seafood, crispy vegetables, and deliciously paired sauces. Every bite was a true gustatory symphony caressing her palate. Each delicate dish was paired with wine, in a brilliantly studied flavor match.

Throughout the meal, the voice guided Jane through the different dishes, describing their composition and preparation with passion. The dishes followed one another: a creamy soup, tender and juicy poultry, skillfully prepared side dishes, and sumptuous desserts.

The voice concluded enthusiastically: "This Christmas meal is more than just a feast, Jane. It is a culinary experience celebrating love, joy, and the magic of this special time of year. Enjoy it fully, Jane, because you deserve this exceptional moment."

Jane found herself savoring every bite, immersing herself in the enchanting atmosphere of this Christmas meal surpassing everything she'd known before. She felt pampered and, in the end, grateful for the opportunity to live such an extraordinary experience.

The voice then took an interest in Jane and curiously asked: "Tell me, Jane, what is your favorite kind of music?" Jane, smiling, enthusiastically answered: "I love jazz!" Immediately, the voice granted her wish and played a piece of slow, refined jazz, with deep bass and crystalline highs filling the bus space with a sweet melody.

Suddenly, under Jane's bewildered gaze, two mirror balls descended synchronously from the ceiling, spreading a myriad of sparkling lights throughout the space. A warm and friendly disco atmosphere quickly settled in, giving the impression of an intimate and convivial celebration.

As the front door of the bus slowly opened, the voice invited Jane to prepare for a surprise. Curious and slightly tipsy, she turned her head toward the entrance and had to hold on to remain standing. She saw an elegant figure, dressed in a black tuxedo with a bow tie, approaching with a feline step and a friendly smile.

The figure approached Jane and said in a soft voice: "Enchanté, Jane. Allow me to invite you to dance to this wonderful music." Jane, surprised but delighted, accepted the invitation with pleasure, not bothering to understand who was behind this white Venetian carnival mask. She simply enjoyed the moment as it presented itself to her. He smelled nice, a mix of vanilla and amber. They headed to the center of the bus as if they had known each other for a long time and let themselves be carried away by the spirited rhythms of the music.

In this warm and festive atmosphere, Jane almost forgot her captivity.

After a few songs, her dance partner withdrew through the door from which he had come. She did not try to follow him to get out of the bus. Anyway, with her drunkenness and heels, she probably avoided sprawling along the beautiful parquet. Besides, she even suspected that there was more than just wine in those magnificent generously-filled glasses during the meal.

"Jane... the time for your Christmas gift has come..." said the voice with a kindly insistence.

Jane looked around again, bewildered, as there were numerous gift boxes scattered here and there.

"Choose the one you want..." the voice suggested.

She hesitated for a few more seconds before approaching a pretty box with metallic wrapping, which shifted from red to purple depending on the angle.

"Go ahead... open your gift..." the voice invited, sharpening her curiosity even further.

Jane gently pulled on a part of the curly bow on top of the box, which came off without resistance. Amused, she found herself unwrapping the rest of the packaging with the eagerness of an impatient child. She had chosen a medium-sized, slightly elongated, black box with her name engraved in gold letters on the lid. An inner smile spread across her face, conscious of the efforts made by the voice to impress her.

She lifted the lid, but it opened slowly, delayed by an air-cushion mechanism designed to prolong the tension of the revelation. Finally, the lid was removed. Jane's face froze, as did her arm still up in the air, holding the lid. Through a thin sheet of white paper, the elongated contours of a pistol with a rough grip and silver barrel emerged.

"Do you like it?" asked the voice.

Jane grasped the pistol and handled it awkwardly. She fumbled to find the mechanism to open the cylinder and eventually succeeded.

"There is only one bullet, Jane..." said the voice, satisfied.

She looked around with the hatred of someone who had been fooled once again.

"I have observed your creativity, Jane... here is your next instruction..." added the voice in a more serious tone.

Jane had no further intention of complying with the orders of this maniac hidden behind this Christmas circus and the altered voice. She hated having her freedom and time stolen without her permission. More than anything, she hated Christmas. And above all, she despised the cowards who hid like larvae behind a distorted voice.

Alcohol helped Jane reach that critical point where the desire to escape surpassed everything else.

She wanted this sadistic game to end as quickly as possible.

She was fully aware that no one would come to her rescue. On this Christmas night, she knew very well that no one was waiting for her. In fact, no one really awaited her in her life in general. If she were to perish that night, few would mourn her. This bitter realization was familiar to her, and this unusual and painful situation only emphasized it with cruel impiety. This was her harsh reality.

She had never made particular efforts to make real friends, people who would have understood and supported her. Friends she would have also helped to grow, as she loved spreading good around her. Often exploited and considered naive, her surroundings had frequently made her feel that she did not belong in their world and, without saying it directly, that she lacked the ruthlessness needed to command respect. Her relationship with her mother would not serve as a lifeline either. Now polite and distant, their relationship kept them on separate paths, each one knowing they would never truly intersect.

Then there was love... She had desperately sought it, multiplying flings, sometimes for one night, only to end up being labeled as an easy girl. Easy and incapable of giving life. Undoubtedly, Jane knew she did not understand the life expected of her, and she mechanically clung to it without passion, without impulse. At an age when some had already built an empire, failed, and rebuilt another, her job in a vibrating cushions factory in the province had never really... made her vibrate.

She sniffled, her nose running. Distractedly, she wiped it with the sleeve of her dress, betraying her abandonment and inability to care for herself with dignity. It was a form of regression to childhood, an escape. She regretted sullying the beautiful dress she had been dressed in to highlight her, in vain. That single bullet seemed like a final message. Tears streamed down her face as she contemplated it, beautiful in its metallic sheath, perfectly nestled in the cylinder, ready to be released with the power to change everything definitively. The sadist who orchestrated this old-fashioned tragedy probably could not imagine how that bullet did not represent a threat to Jane, but rather the key to a door toward her complete escape.

"You're crying, Jane..." observed the voice, somewhat annoyed.

She did not respond. She closed the cylinder, ensuring the bullet was properly in place. She introduced the barrel into her mouth, barely opening it, deep inside, holding the weapon diagonally with her thumb on the trigger to effectively aim at the brain. One detail saddened her: that the blood spray would be invisible with all the red already present in the décor. But at least, if the barrel was well-aligned as she supposed, she would have the pride of sending part of her brain splattering against the ceiling. Then, falling onto one of the prettily decorated little Christmas trees, it would serve as a garland.

"Jane, what are you doing?" asked the voice without waiting.

Jane looked at the screens broadcasting her image. She saw herself from the front and profile. This allowed her to better adjust the angle of the barrel in her mouth to ensure hitting the target. Jane liked precision. Was she ready to pull the trigger? Yes, of course. At this exact moment, all the resentment against herself, meticulously nurtured over time, surfaced and tightened her throat: her hopes, her disillusions, her failed life. In truth, life had not wronged her. It was rather she who had not done what was necessary to build the life she expected.

The life she dreamed of but never had the courage to build. That, she knew perfectly well. And no one would be there tonight to tell her that everything was still possible. To top it off, she could not bear this role of a docile toy in the hands of a madman. She had no pity for that idiot Jane who had found nothing better than to get on that lousy bus, not to mention on Christmas Eve.

She slowly closed her eyes, ready to welcome that lovely golden-clad bullet into herself.

"JANE!" yelled the voice, shaking the entire bus compartment, before trailing off into a fit of coughing, as if it had swallowed the wrong way.

Intrigued, Jane opened her eyes.

"Put the gun down..." pleaded the voice.

Jane mentally sifted through her contacts, wondering who the idiot behind this voice might be, who evidently cared for her. This luxurious outfit, this festive dinner, and now this plea to stay alive... Yet, she could think of no one who might care about her to this extent. On the other hand, nearly all her contacts could have wanted to torment her to the point that death became an option.

"What is this bullet for then?" she asked mockingly, speaking with difficulty as she removed the barrel from her mouth.

The voice remained silent for a few seconds, as if trying to wiggle out of its own trap.

"You can go out, Jane..." murmured the voice, now sinister, as the bus doors opened and the lights slowly dimmed.

Jane's eyes blinked several times, trying to adjust to the oppressive darkness that enveloped her. Her heart pounded frenetically in her chest as she cautiously moved towards the central doors. Each step echoed in the silence, resonating along with her heartbeats of fear.

Holding her weapon tightly, Jane took a few more steps. But the click of her heels seemed like a deadly alert. Carefully, she removed them, letting them slide silently to the floor.

The door did not lead to the outside world. There were no reassuring lights, no swirling snowflakes, no wisps of wind. She had been transported elsewhere, far from the city, far from the winding road on the hill. The exterior of the bus was stunningly silent.

A scream of terror threatened to burst from Jane's throat, but she suppressed it just in time. Instead, a cold sweat beaded on her forehead, trailing down her neck, slipping into the folds of her décolleté. Other drops of cold sweat also bead from her armpits down her sides.

Reaching the double doors, she began to perceive a breath, a raspy respiration that chilled her blood.

Her heart pounding wildly, Jane summoned her courage and advanced, one step at a time, into the suffocating darkness. The raspy breathing swirled around her, invisible, elusive. Each wheezing breath sent shivers of fright down her spine.

The fear squeezed her from all sides, creating an indescribable anxiety in her mind. Her senses were on high alert, tracking the slightest sign of danger, but this presence remained elusive, toying with her in this darkened atmosphere.

Suddenly, a cold draft swept through her hair, making her clammy skin shiver. She felt irregular breaths brush against her neck, slide down her spine, like phantom fingers seeking contact. Her breath caught in her throat, as tingles of horror coursed through her frail body.

She wanted to scream, to flee, but she was trapped in this impenetrable darkness, powerless against this invisible predator. Her trembling hand tightened its grip on the pistol, but she couldn't shoot at a target she couldn't see.

The tension was at its peak, every fiber of her being saturated with unbearable anxiety. The raspy breathing grew more intense, insinuating its sinister venom into her already shaken mind. Jane was on the verge of breaking, ready to succumb to the terror that threatened to completely overwhelm her.

Spatial references escaped her, and Jane found herself disoriented, unable to determine the current position of the bus. The environment's contours blurred, melding the boundaries of reality. She was trapped in a dark labyrinth where the perception of space had vanished.

The raspy breath drew closer, intensifying with every moment, intertwining with Jane's flesh in a terrifying yet oddly sensual manner. Like a serpent slithering through the dark recesses of her mind, it grazed her skin, triggering a cascade of horror and excitement mingling in a macabre dance.

She could almost feel the irregular breaths caressing her arms, slowly ascending along her neck, enveloping her in an invisible embrace. The darkness fueled her imagination, amplifying the sensations, making them more tangible, more intense.

Each fleeting contact evoked a wave of disgust mingled with a curious fascination. The paradox of terror and attraction kept her in a state of uncertainty and forbidden excitement.

She felt at the mercy of this indefinable presence, torn between the urge to escape and the perverse desire to discover the identity of her invisible assailant. The tension was at its peak, her mind writhing in a whirlwind of desire and fear, unsure where to place itself in this troubling duality.

Each wheezing breath sent shivers coursing through Jane from head to toe, triggering disturbing echoes within her being. She felt as if each breath carried a dark promise, an invitation to plunge into the abyss of the unknown.

Despite the terror coursing through her, she couldn't help but be captivated by this horrifying tension, as if the darkness itself had awakened a dark, hidden part of her. Her body responded with a peculiar complicity, vibrating under the intangible caresses of this invisible presence.

In this moment, inextricably intertwined with terror and sensuality, she felt she was at a crossroads, on the sharp edge between life and death, between safety and abandonment. A part of her wanted to yield to this morbid seduction, to be carried away by the depths of the forbidden, while another part of her fiercely resisted, fighting for her survival and escape.

This tension closed in on her like an enveloping spider web, this enchanting terror pushing her to move forward, to succumb, offered to the surrounding darkness.

The hoarse breath persisted, closer and closer, in this macabre dance between horror and seduction. She found herself at the edge of the abyss, ready to step over the threshold that would open the doors to intense and dangerous pleasure, or perhaps, just maybe, an escape to an unsuspected freedom.

THE FEAR BUS

The Light

Jane instinctively closed her eyes, but even the darkness couldn't suppress the powerful lights glaring at her, blinding her, and casting the threatening shadows of the police officers in front of her. Her hands rose as a visor above her eyes as she tried to make out their faces.

"What is this?" she murmured, surprised and anxious, but the response was immediate.

"DO NOT MOVE!" bellowed Commander Partol in a rough and powerful voice, akin to a wild roar. His team spread out in an arc around her, their weapons aimed directly at her, ready to strike. Their labored breaths filled the air, amplifying the palpable tension. Adam and Kevin stood back, their exhausted figures evidence of a frantic chase. Adam straightened up with difficulty, desperately searching for air.

"What's happening here?" Jane tried to understand the situation, lost and disoriented in this suffocating nightmare.

The commander took a step forward, legs apart and fists clenched on his hips, exuding a sense of unyielding power.

"I am Commander Partol," he introduced himself, puffing up his chest to show his bravery to his troops, and emphasizing his name as if planting a flag on unknown land. "You are under arrest," he announced in an icy tone, pointing an accusatory finger at her while covering his mouth with his other hand. "ARREST HER!"

The commander's men cautiously advanced towards Jane, their weapons aimed, their gazes filled with astonishment and terror. Out of breath, Adam tried to reassure Jane, while Kevin struggled to regain control of his breathing.

"FASTER!" roared the commander to galvanize his troops, exhibiting apparent bravado.

"Wait, what's going on? Why are you arresting me?" Jane was lost, searching for answers in this chaos.

The police officers quickly approached, gripping her firmly, an arm on each side. Jane struggled, but their hold was relentless.

"STOP! YOU'RE HURTING ME!" she screamed, feeling her bloody arms burn painfully.

The commander smirked with satisfaction, savoring the scene as if it were a personal triumph. "I'm the one arresting you! Damien, read her her rights."

In a monotone and hesitant voice, the officer began to recite the suspect's rights, thus formalizing her arrest.

Jane looked at her bloody arms, her face desperate, seeking explanations in Commander Partol's malignant smile.

"What have you done to me?" she implored in a pleading tone, as the threatening shadow of the thriller took root around her, dragging her world into an infernal spiral of tension and mystery.

Commander Partol showed her his phone, held in selfie mode.

With apprehension, Jane gazed at her image on the phone's screen. Horror gripped her as she discovered the nightmare etched on her face. Blood smeared her lips, cheeks, and had spread into her hair, creating a nightmarish appearance.

Jane looked up at the commander, an expression of shock and incomprehension etched on her face. "What happened? Why am I covered in blood?"

Commander Partol's smug smile transformed into a malicious gleam in his eyes. "You don't remember, Jane?" he said, bringing the phone screen closer to Jane's face.

Shock overwhelmed her as fragmented memories of that infernal night came back to her. Flashes of violent altercations, screams, fire, the metallic taste of blood in her mouth, all mixed in her troubled mind.

"No... it's not possible..." she stammered, torn between doubt and the harsh reality presented to her.

The commander and the officers surrounding her observed her dismay with unhealthy curiosity. The phone screen reflected a terrifying image, as if she no longer recognized a part of herself.

The tension escalated, and Jane felt the trap closing inexorably around her. Questions raced through her mind, but the answers seemed to dissolve in a maze of shadows and lies.

Keeping his weapon pointed at her, Commander Partol approached, his voice oozing with manipulative venom. "It's too late to deny. We have visual witnesses. Your image, your voice are everywhere, and probably your DNA too. You're caught."

This extravagant setup filled her with anger. She knew she was innocent. Deep down, she felt that something darker and more complex was behind all this. But how could she prove her innocence when everything seemed so overwhelming? She started shaking her arms, then her entire body to break free from the two officers holding her but failed. The officers gripped her even more firmly and lifted her off the ground to prevent any escape attempt.

"Listen to me! I was kidnapped! For endless hours, I fought to escape, desperately trying to flee this hell... My phone, he had locked everything to prevent me from calling for help... At one point, I managed to escape, in a dark night ablaze with fire... But he found me, always on my heels, giving me no respite... I beg you, you must help me!"

Her words, laden with terror, resonated in that dark place lost in the middle of nowhere. She had thought that freedom was finally within her grasp, but now she found herself at the mercy of other predators, this time in uniform. The police officers, meant to protect her, seemed to have become her worst nightmares, plunging her into an abyss of mistrust.

As she relived every traumatic moment with horror, her gaze scrutinized the complicit faces before her. A cold shiver ran down her spine as she realized that her ordeal was far from over. Her heart skipped beats, like a malfunctioning clock, as her trembling, bloody hands begged Commander Partol for help.

Kevin discreetly moved towards the commander, eager to get a closer look at Jane's face. His eyes fixed on her with a disturbing mix of disgust and fascination. With a calm but firm gesture, the commander pulled him back, while Adam made insistent signs for him to stay back, not to interfere with the action, and to let law enforcement do their job.

Jane was handcuffed and taken to a van specially designed for transporting highly dangerous suspects. Colleagues from a neighboring department had reacted swiftly to the commander's urgent call, sending the vehicle in record time. It was an unusual situation, a high-risk mission in a place they rarely frequented. The atmosphere was electric, and all officers were on high alert, ready to respond to any sign of agitation.

Once at the Cassay police station, Jane's custody began under explosive conditions. She scratched violently at anyone who approached her, throwing punches and overthrowing everything in her path. Her screams echoed through the corridors, making the veins in her neck vibrate. The police struggled to restrain her during the photo session. With her face covered in blood and hair matted with dried blood, Jane offered a disconcerting resistance for a young woman of her seemingly ordinary stature.

The law enforcement officers had to redouble their efforts to clean her, but each attempt at washing was an arduous battle. She fought like a caged animal, exuding a desperate savagery. Her physical strength, astonishingly surprising, did not match her frail appearance in the slightest.

Everyone sensed that Jane was not an ordinary criminal, but something far darker and more complex. Her disturbing actions and fierce resistance seemed to defy the laws of nature itself, plunging the police into an abyss of concern and perplexity.

She was placed in the interrogation room after refusing to speak to the lawyer assigned to her. The interrogation room resembled a nightmarish vision, plunged into a gloomy semi-darkness. Worn-out neon lights hung from the ceiling, casting a flickering and sinister glow on the damp-stained walls. The smell of disinfectant barely masked the stuffy, musty air of this decrepit room, where time seemed to have stood still for years.

At the back of this dark room, Jane sat, stiffened by the handcuffs on her wrists and ankles that kept her to her chair to prevent any violent movement. Her face, marked by previous battles, displayed a hardened expression, her eyes holding an inscrutable glimmer. Across from her, Commander Partol sat at the other end of the table, surrounded by a stack of hastily gathered, crumpled documents. His gaze, sharp and unwavering, sought to unravel the mystery surrounding this enigmatic young woman.

Cassay was a small, peaceful town that rarely saw such scenes. The police station itself had seen more glorious days, but the interrogation room had been forgotten by time. Signs of wear, cracks in the walls, and outdated equipment told a story of neglect and disinterest for this sinister place.

A half-dozen, anxious and attentive police officers were present, underscoring the gravity of the case. The oppressive silence was broken only by the regular buzzing of the tired neon lights. The atmosphere was electric, everyone holding their breath, waiting for the slightest move from Jane, ready to act at the slightest deviation.

Deep inside, Jane couldn't believe it... but who had it out for her?

In front of her, Commander Partol began reading the documents in a monotone voice, like a long list of groceries.

"You are suspected... when I say suspected... we have bodies, images, and a considerable amount of fingerprints and DNA samples are being collected every minute... in short. You are suspected of ending the lives of Paul Kowalski, the eldest son from a first marriage of our mayor Igor

Kowalski. Of Roger, the only homeless person known to our services. We were just looking for him to invite him to the city's charity Christmas Eve dinner. Of Miguel Figueira, a driver for eighteen years at Victoria Transport, and seven passengers of bus number 8, whom you massacred and left on the sidewalk. Of Igor Kowalski, the mayor of Cassay, recently re-elected for the second time in a row. Of Louis Fermann and Lucas Belich, two childhood friends. Of the four passengers on bus number 3. Of Gabriel Kowalski and his sister, Alice Kowalski, both children of Mayor Igor Kowalski. Of Annette Kowalski, Igor Kowalski's sister, who came specifically from abroad to spend Christmas Eve with the family. And finally, of Samuel Keller, the maître d'hôtel of the Astor restaurant..."

The commander paused, afflicted by the long list he had just recited aloud. The faces of the police officers in the room were dismayed, but they tried to maintain their composure out of professionalism. Jane heard without truly listening.

"This is what we know. These are the first elements we have. Are there perhaps others?" the commander asked as he stood up and stretched as if getting out of bed.

Nonchalant, he approached Jane and, taking her by the chin, turned her face towards him.

"You've scored at an international level, Jane. Thanks to you, the small town of Cassay will achieve fame!" he said menacingly. But deep down, he saw himself already parading down the main avenue in a convertible, receiving the crowd's applause under a shower of confetti, as if he had just walked on the Moon.

"And you are going to explain everything to me in detail, minute by minute," he added, bringing his face closer to Jane's to better intimidate her. But he almost kissed her, out of gratitude. Jane was his moment, his pinnacle, his winning lottery ticket.

"I treated them! He forced me to treat them! I didn't know anything about it!" Jane explained desperately.

"You massacred them, systematically, Jane," insisted Commander Partol, emphasizing the word "systematically."

"NO! NO!" she screamed again, struggling, trying to get up to leave the room.

"Calm down! Alright. Let's suppose your kidnapper existed. Let's suppose. How did he know about the blue rose, Jane?" the commander asked, certain he was about to play his trump card.

Humiliated at being taken for something she wasn't, Jane spat in his face. She was determined not to give in to his sadistic game, just as she hadn't given in to that of the voice. She held the promise she had made to herself: no one would dictate what to do anymore.

Commander Partol, seized by uncontrollable rage at Jane's affront, immediately raised his arm, ready to strike the young woman violently to make her pay for her provocative act. However, before he could carry out his plan, one of the officers, used to discreetly managing his superior's excesses, stepped between them, intercepting the imminent blow.

The officer gave the commander an intense stare, without a word, but his gaze expressed an unwavering refusal, clearly signaling that violence was not an option. The commander, frustrated and visibly annoyed by this interference, reconsidered, regaining his senses.

In tense silence, he returned to his place on the other side of the table, signaling his discontent with a sharp jaw movement. His ego had taken a hit, but he knew he had to pull himself together, stay calm, and continue playing his role as an impartial investigator.

He fixed his gaze on Jane for a long moment, then snapped his fingers for the evidence to be brought in.

The police officers started playing the audio and video recordings for Jane, which unfolded like a waking nightmare. Each image revealed a terrifying facet of herself that she did not recognize. Horrific scenes followed one another: she dragged bodies, slit throats, disemboweled victims, acting like someone possessed by a dark force.

The sound of her voice, recorded during these abominable acts, hinted at a troubling duality. At times, she spoke with a soft, almost calm voice, as if speaking to someone absent on the buses where she had committed her crimes. Then, her tone changed, becoming deep and sinister, as if a malevolent presence had taken over her.

It was both terrifying and bewildering. How could she be both the person she knew herself to be, an ordinary young woman, and this ruthless killer who spread terror in the town?

The spectators in the interrogation room were chilled with fear, even the seasoned officers who had seen many horrors throughout their careers. The degree of violence in the images was unbearable, almost inhuman, and defied any rational explanation.

Jane herself was frightened by what she saw and heard. She felt like a stranger to these horrible scenes, as if someone else had taken control of her body. The idea that her hands could have committed such acts appalled her and plunged her into deep distress.

The images finally stopped, leaving a heavy silence in the room. The officers looked at Jane with distrust, searching for answers to questions that seemed beyond all understanding.

Commander Partol spoke in a harsh, accusatory tone. "What do you have to say in your defense, Jane? These recordings seem to overwhelmingly show your involvement in these atrocities. How can you explain this?"

Jane's eyes scanned the room, stopping on each face that scrutinized her, as tears streamed from her eyes in torrents, stifling the sobs that choked her. She appeared like a broken soul, abandoned and disoriented, desperately seeking a hint of understanding and compassion in the gazes that fixed upon her.

Her gaze met that of the officer who had stopped the violent gesture of Commander Partol. In his eyes, she found a glimmer of kindness, a spark of empathy that gave her comfort for a moment. This simple gesture of support reminded her that she was not entirely alone in facing this storm of devastating accusations.

However, the rest of the room was filled with a cold and accusatory atmosphere. The police officers scrutinized Jane's every reaction, looking for signs of guilt in her tears and wandering eyes.

But in her heart, Jane knew she was innocent. She didn't understand how these recordings showed her as the author of these atrocities. Something dark and mysterious seemed to have taken control of her being, manipulating her like a soulless puppet.

The memories she had of those moments were blurry, as if she had been plunged into a waking nightmare from which she could not fully emerge. She clung to the idea that perhaps there was a rational explanation behind all this, a hidden truth that she needed to discover to prove her innocence.

But for now, in this oppressive interrogation room, she felt vulnerable and overwhelmed by the crushing pressure of the accusations. Her tears flowed freely, revealing deep distress, as if she were imploring to be freed from the nightmare tormenting her.

Jane was far from being the bloodthirsty killer that the evidence seemed to depict. She was an ordinary young woman, with simple dreams and hopes, whose life had been upturned by inexplicable events. That night, for the Christmas Eve she was preparing to spend alone once again, she just wanted to go home to rest and clear her mind in front of her favorite series.

In a final effort to resist the wave of despair that threatened to engulf her, she raised her head and looked Commander Partol in the eyes, as a challenge. Despite the fear gnawing at her, a glimmer appeared in her eyes. She would fight, she would fight until the end to restore the truth. Deep down, she knew she was not this savage murderer that the recordings seemed to depict.

THE FEAR BUS

Epilogue

The next day, Kevin woke up exhausted but filled with a sense of pride that warmed his heart despite the fatigue. The events of the previous day had been grueling, but he knew that they had helped to stop a series of horrific murders that had terrorized the city. Every minute replayed in his mind, reminding him of the importance of his contribution to this very special mission.

Commander Partol's advice still echoed in his mind. The latter had encouraged him to consider a career in the police, recognizing in him the qualities necessary for success in this field. Kevin was flattered to have been recognized and encouraged by an experienced officer like the commander. It wasn't with his direct superior, Adam, that he could have hoped for such encouragement.

He got up to make the morning coffee. A wave of frustration hit him when he discovered that the coffee packet was split open, spilling its precious black powder. With a nonchalant gesture, he tried to salvage what was left by scooping some of the scattered coffee off the counter and pouring it into a glass that desperately needed a good wash.

As he moved towards the kettle, he realized it was completely out of order, refusing to turn on despite his multiple attempts. Disappointment added to frustration, and he abandoned the idea of making coffee for now.

Dragging his feet, he went back to his bedroom, leaving behind the mess and inconvenience of the kitchen. On the way, he couldn't help but think that he should take a moment to tidy up and fix some things in his apartment. But for now, he needed a little respite.

In his bedroom, the atmosphere was more soothing, though slightly chaotic too. The walls, adorned with posters of his favorite games and iconic characters, seemed to tell a fantastic story to anyone who cared to listen. Shelves filled with figurines, game consoles, controllers, and game boxes formed a true virtual Aladdin's cave. Cables and wires intertwined like tangled snakes, giving the impression that every corner of the room was connected to a digital universe.

He flopped onto his bed, his gaze lost in the ceiling, wondering if his morning misfortune was a sign of a tougher day ahead.

Grateful faces, warm thanks from his colleagues, and the commander Partol's encouragements haunted his thoughts. These memories might mark the turning point in his life that he had been eagerly waiting for.

Sitting on the edge of his bed again, Kevin recalled all the times he had to remain calm during this intense chase.

The sense of accomplishment mingled with the idea of training to join the police ranks. This prospect filled him with excitement and apprehension.

As the sun slowly rose on the horizon, he went back to the living room and absentmindedly turned on the television. After the coffee fiasco, he decided to try orange juice. Surely, he had some left. He headed towards the refrigerator when he was caught by a live broadcast from the continuous news channel, reporting from the scene of the previous day's events. They almost talked about him.

"A sordid car chase terrorized the whole city of Cassay in the north of the country during the night of December 24 to 25.

While its inhabitants were celebrating Christmas Eve, Jane Kowalski, the mayor's wife, was arrested after a bloody rampage through the city's streets. The young woman, in her thirties and mother of two children, successively hijacked two public buses, massacring more than twenty people, according to a real-time updated count.

The small city of Cassay had never before experienced such an incident. Local police forces managed to put an end to this murderous madness with the support of a professional drone pilot, before the arrival of special forces.

The suspect, who had been monitored in a specialized center for many years, had been allowed to attend the Christmas Eve dinner with her family after the insistence of her husband Igor Kowalski and their children. She eventually surrendered without resistance to the police after starting to eat the corpses of her victims at the end of her macabre journey. Initial hearings and psychiatric examinations of the suspect suggest that she suffers from a dissociative identity disorder, which worsened to the point of completely abolishing her discernment at the time of the events. According to the experts responsible for the investigation, this state might make criminal responsibility uncertain. A psychological support unit has been set up for the families of the numerous victims..."

Kevin, fascinated by this incredible story, turned off the television. His ears were still ringing too loudly from the previous night's noises. He tossed the remote, which bounced off the couch and fell to the floor. Amused and fatalistic, he took a few steps towards the refrigerator, ready to open the door when a loud knock echoed through his apartment's intercom.

Who would dare to disturb him at this early hour? Fame would have to wait until he poured himself some orange juice to wake up. He opened the refrigerator; the bottle no longer had its cap. There was a finger of juice left at the bottom, offering itself to him as the ultimate reward. He grabbed the bottle and drank it directly, letting out an "Aaaaahh!" of satisfaction followed by a small burp, as the intercom buzzed again.

"Alright, alright!" he mumbled, dragging his feet over to the intercom handset which he picked up.

"Good morning, Kevin..." said a deep and benevolent voice, mixed with a burst of shrill static.

THE FEAR BUS

THE END

121

About the Author

Discover the captivating universe of PAUL TOSKIAM, the master of the extraordinary infiltrating the ordinary. With a voracious pleasure for turning mundane situations into thrilling adventures, he will make you reevaluate your certainties and completely shake up your perspective.

Forget about traditional patterns because with PAUL TOSKIAM, you will be drawn into extraordinary plots where tension is palpable on every page turned. The heroes and villains are not who you think they are. It's what will drive you crazy, but also what you'll love.

But that's not all, subtle and irresistible humor is one of PAUL TOSKIAM's trademarks. His characters come to life with realism, becoming endearing and unpredictable, adding a unique touch to each story.

www.ingramcontent.com/pod-product-compliance
Lightning Source LLC
Chambersburg PA
CBHW031426150726
47989CB00002B/823